The Daug
Pendle

By

Darcy Boyd Mahoney

For Tracey and Bogart.
Neither of whom, it has to be said, has shown any interest in reading this finished version of the book!

Bogarts' excuse is he's a dog. At least I hope that would be his excuse.

Traceys' would be that she's read earlier versions and unfortunately the story no longer holds any surprises for her.
That is of course true.
Tracey, I love you...
Will you marry me?
X

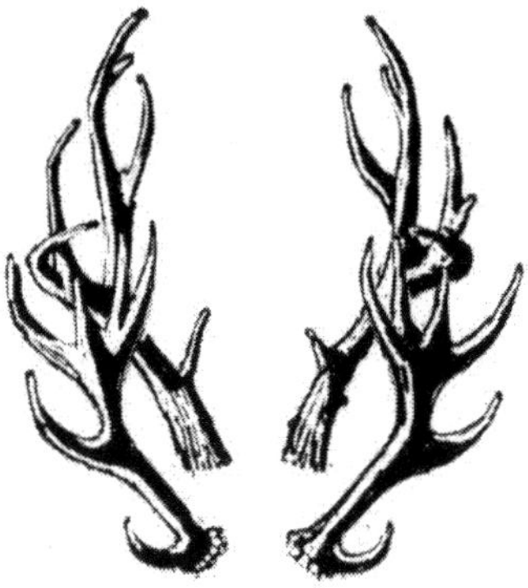

COPYRIGHT INFORMATION

The Daughters of Pendle

Published 2022 by typingmonkey

Cover design: typingmonkey

Original Cover Painting: 'A Walk in the Woods'

ISBN 978-1-7398494-0-5

Prologue

Dark clouds swamp the proud plateau as a heavy mist shrouds the steep flanks of the surrounding hillscape. A wooden signpost leans, crooked, into the spikey hedgerow. The carved pointer stretches toward the forbidding skyline.

Pendle

It is 1564

Horses strike out across the bleak horizon, the snarling beasts as thirsty for the quarry as the bitter faced riders. These are witchfinders and they are hungry for fire and flame.

As they course through the scrubland the group splits into two as the roar of the hooves and the snorting of the horses fills the air with dark, angry anticipations.

In a shallow crevasse on the side of the greyed knoll the fog clings to a small patch of woodland; cold, dull, and gloomy. The crashing hooves explode from the dense mist as this fierce company of riders tear along the rough road and into the dirt streets of a tiny hamlet. They quickly dismount to surround the doorway of a rustic cottage.

The other troop follow a gravel road down into the bowl of the grand landscape, racing toward a large, lone manor house.

The doors to both abodes are shattered from their hinges as soldiers, some more nervous than others, prepare to enter.

Inside the cottage, some old women are immediately cornered and despite shouted threats and angry protestations are manacled quickly as their papers and books are swept from tables into a pile in the middle of the rustic, wiccan room. The Overseer; the Witchfinder General, gives the order to burn it as the women are dragged from the home. Some younger women, clutching the hands of scruffy children, scurry from the site.

At the Manor House, hesitant men are passed by as clearer minded soldiers force their way deeper into the building; searching the rooms as more doors are smashed from their frames.

Bursting from the shadows; shrieking defenders, hidden by makeshift shields and panels; men and women attack the insurgents, brandishing household utensils as weapons. Their efforts are easily subdued as the soldiers chase several cowled women who head down cellar steps into darkness and a long stone tunnel.

In the tunnel one of the fleeing women turns and raises her hand as her fingers dance in a studied manipulation. The soldier chasing at her heels stops in his tracks and panics under her gaze. Followed by the less superstitious, he is pushed past and he drops his oil lamp setting himself alight. The woman turns and continues into the darkness as the man, ablaze, also turns to run screaming from the passage.

At the mouth of the cellar steps other soldiers fall back aghast at the appearance of this burning man as he screams of the witchcraft unleashed upon him. Their own Captain; caped and cowled himself, passes by these now stuttering thugs, and is calm in his descending of the steps as he follows in the wake of the women and his pursuing officers.

At the far end of the tunnel the officers are pushing their way through a heavy, wooden, metal-strapped, dungeon door, and they pry it open as their enigmatic superior approaches and he steps through into the dark room. Flickering torch light bounces from the cold, damp, walls. The old women stand defiant, their backs against the doors of some protected nook.

The captain approaches the women; behind him the room fills with his men.

Woman : (as the Captain approaches she again raises her hands...) **You will never know the power of creation or...**

He slaps the crone to the ground and his men rush to take hold of her as she and all the women are aggressively subdued.

He watches calmly as they are dragged from the room. He looks about this hallowed space then approaches the small, gnarled wooden doors in the wall. He lifts a clasp releasing them and they swing open. A shallow alcove; three shelves filled with books and loose papers falls under his brooding gaze. His men come to his side and start to grab at the objects.

Officer : (to the other men) **Burn it, burn it all...**

The Captain : (soft, mellifluous tones) **No. We will keep these.**

His officer looks quizzical.

The Captain : **For the historical record.**

The order is accepted and the books, papers and trinkets are thrown into a hessian sack. The room empties and quickly falls silent. Alone, the Captain, once again considers the torch-lit space, he breaths in, savouring some essence in the atmosphere before following the others back into the dark tunnel.

In the blinding daylight, the soldiers now flank the manacled women as they are marched across the scrubby grasslands.

The more superstitious among the soldiery are careful not to catch the eye of any of the women.

They continue as the women weary.

Somewhere in the distance a line of gibbets stands stark in the barren landscape.

Stood on the edge of the platform the women, strung now by their necks and with chains hanging from their ankles, wait silently.

From the saddle of his horse the Witchfinder General, the hooded Captain similarly comfortable behind him, addresses the women. They are watched by some unseen viewers who hide in the long grass.

Witchfinder General : **You have proven yourselves to be unreliable in your accounts and representations of your dealings with the darkest arts. You have one last chance to redeem yourselves in the eyes of the one true power and light... Don't waste it.** (He nods toward the leader of the women) **Please...**

Woman : (she looks beaten. She lifts her weary head...) **It is the truth...there is, only one true power,** (she builds in fervour) **and to our daughters I beg you, never let weak men turn you from Her attentions. It is not the strong who you should fear but the weak and angry who are compelled to control...**

The Witchfinder General has heard enough and he calmly signals to the hangman who pulls a lever and the front of the platform falls away. The women drop as the muffled cries of children are windswept from the long grasses.

The Daughters of Pendle

It is 1998

Flaming torch-light dances on her flesh. It soaks into the rough, dark fabric which, for the moment, hides his nakedness from her.

He mutters under his breath. Strange words. Old words.

Moving his hand down to the small of her back his fingertips lightly brush her skin before he plants his hand firmly and pulls her half naked body forward, toward him.

Reciting still, he stares into her nervous eyes and dips his head in a nod—a subtle question. Scared and nervous, she nods back.

She turns her face away from his.

He slips his free hand between the folds of the dark cloak that drapes across his shoulders and throws the garment open.

Her hand comes up to her face, over her eyes, trying to hide from the event.

The hooded cloak slides off his shoulders.

As the torchlight flickers, he flexes and tenses as animal instincts and passions surge through him, vital, erect.

He chants the incantation louder now as he lifts his own hand and, grabbing her chin, turns her face back towards him, forcing her gaze to meet his. He pauses, then with a gasp he pushes toward her...

Her : (frantic) **No... No....I'm not ready, I'm sorry.**

Him : **Oh for fuck sake..!** (he stops immediately)

The crowd's gasp fills the air.

Him : (calling an instruction) **Lights.**

A small click echoes forth and tired strip lights stutter into half-life. She reaches quickly and covers her nakedness as the disapprovals of the cloaked and cowled gathering resound about this perfunctory, beige, hall.

He, pale and pudgier than expected, stands frustrated. Totally naked, with his small stick-like erection bobbing before him, he angrily addresses the seated crowd.

Him : (stern) **Not good enough...** (sterner) **Not good enough.**

He turns to see her cowering at the side of the cheap modular staging. He has no sympathy.

Him : **Sacrifice...** (he stares at her) **Belief....**

Then, a voice from the crowd.

Voice : **Make her do it.**

Him : (he spins angrily toward the voice) **Have you learnt nothing...?**

He turns back to continue berating the girl.

Him : (disappointment, less anger) **Without compliance the ceremony means nothing, can achieve nothing.**

A study in contrition, she grabs the rest of her garb and quietly slinks from the stage.

He watches her departure before spinning back to address the congregation, his failing erection swinging half limp in the gloom.

Him : (calming himself) **You know the master shall be with us in a few days' time. And, although he is aware we are a young, re-formed coven, I know he hopes we shall show the strengths of our forebears.** (He struts proudly across the stage) **The belief of our forebears. The freedom of sacrifice...** (he puts his hands together and brings his index fingers up to rest on his chin) **You know, it is the greatest sacrifices which will reap the greatest rewards.** (he nods into the crowd) **Ultimate sacrifice will reap the ultimate reward, will it not? The master**

has such a gift to bestow upon any of you willing to demonstrate this understanding. We'll be talking more about that later. Think about it.

He claps his hands together. Reinvigorated, again he struts across the stage.

Him : **Now then, as I am sure you are aware, I am now, 'Rite bound'. Bearing what I have said in mind, I would appreciate a volunteer to see out this final important stage of the ceremony... Anyone?... You, of course, won't be bound to the contract...This is about releasing me from it. Now, anybody?**

He looks, hopefully, out into the crowd of hoods and masks. A slim wrist rises from the sea of dark weft.

His hopeful expression drops away and with a tired gasp he looks to the floor.

Him : (resigned) **Ah, Michael**. (another sigh) **Lights.!**

Monmouth, Wales. **Saturday 24th Oct**

The Queens Head

A group of friends are halfway through a boozy night out and are heading to the next pub. Like any bunch of lads, they are laughing, joking, and taking the piss out of each other.

Ariff is at the front. Very good looking, he exudes a relaxed, easy-going charm and friendly sense of humour; even strangers met in passing get a smile and empathetic nod.

This rowdy troop is walking towards another lively pub. An abundance of fancy-dressed revellers pours past in both directions and the guys weave between the drunken fairies, zombies and witches as they make their own way to the door of 'The Queens Head'.

Ariff, at the front of the wraggle, peers through the small leaded windows of the ancient pub and spies a bevy of sexy, fancy-dressed fairies at the bar. He turns back to the guys and, with a broad smile, signals his recommendation that this is indeed, the greatest pub in all the world.

At the back of this disparate procession Brekk is trying to illicit some intelligent conversation from the polite Graham.

Graham : (distracted, but making effort) **Yeah well, I guess it is all relative.**

Brekk : (seeing the choice of venue) **Oh for fuck. We won't be able to hear ourselves think.**

Graham doesn't look as upset.

Brekk looks through the small window as he approaches the door and sees the sexy revellers.

Brekk : (unimpressed) **Why's he always got to choose the noisiest pub?**

Graham tries not to look too happy as he pulls a resigned, conciliatory expression back toward Brekk. Then as he turns toward the held open pub door his face fills with joy and he marches toward the party that Ariff has instantly ignited at the bar.

Brekk, nonplussed, follows him in but heads toward a less busy section of the long wooden counter, struggles grumpily and distastefully between some drinkers and then edges onto a sticky bar stool.

He tries to capture one of the bar girls' attention.

The evening progresses, the guys flirting and laughing as girls come and go. Brekk, still defiant, sits away. He tries to find intelligent conversation from the drinkers around him but is rebuffed at every attempt.

Girl1 : **It's not Halloween though is it? It's next week.**

Girl2 : **What, really?**

Overhearing the girls discussing the date and events of the evening he leans across to offer his thoughts.

Brekk : **The actual date is of little concern to the landlord.**

One of the girls cocks her head in interest.

Brekk : (bolstered, turning theatrical) **No, the brewer's calendar dictates the celebrations, and a false 'Sowwin' angers false gods** (he lifts his glass) **and brings forth false spirits.**

He holds his glass before him like a sacred chalice, his eyes sparkling with performance.

Girl : (dull) **Oh. Is that why Big Brother isn't on?**

Brekk : **What ? Um, I don't...**

Deflated and disappointed he turns away as the girls descend into a cackling conversation about some 'hot', 'celebrity', arsehole.

Brekk looks into the mirror behind the spirit bottles opposite him and considers his face, a small look of disappointment crossing his features when a loud laugh breaks his concentration.

His friends. He glowers across and notices that the handsome Ariff has his arm around the tight waist of a strikingly beautiful, and smiling, fancy-dress fairy. Brekk shakes his head dismissively as he turns back to his half pint of bitter and lifts it to his lips. A firm hand is suddenly on his shoulder and he coughs the mouthful back into his glass.

Mac : **What the fuck are you doing over here? I thought you said you were up for it tonight.**

Brekk : (wiping the drips from his mouth and chin) **Well, no one said anything about this...** (he waves blindly about him) **fucking nonsense. 'A quiet drink' you said. I thought we'd be able to talk.**

Mac : **Well...** (he considers the options) ...**we just got lucky, I guess. Anyway, I thought you liked all of this mystical stuff.**

Brekk : (impugned) **No, not this fancy-dress bollocks.** (he sees and seizes his chance) **But, it is fascinating to see how society still plays with notions of the metaphysical, especially when it comes to self-empowerment.**

His own enthusiasm is stymied as he watches Mac's interest dissolve.

Mac : (looking across as more of the fairies' friends have joined the group) **Come on, Ariff's on good form.**

Brekk : (dejected) **Oh, really? Has he managed to string a sentence together?**

Mac : (gives Brekk a small look of disappointment) **Now, now!**

Brekk : (resigned) **Oh, I'll be over in a minute, I'll just get..**

Mac : (already heading back toward the gang) **Great, great...**

Brekk, disheartened, discards the glass along the bar. He catches the eye of one of the bar girls.

Brekk : (he ventures a small smile) **A rum, please.**

Without any visible hint of warmth or pleasure, she takes a glass tumbler from the shelf.

Brekk : (his smile falls away and he looks across at the braying mob that makes up his group of friends) **Better make it a large one.**

Elsewhere

Old, wizened hands move over a boiling broth and arcane words fill the flame-dappled air. Young, taut bodies drip with oily preparations and nervous sweat. A haze of voices and panorama of piercing eyes focus intently as a chorus builds to crescendo and the imbued words infect the libidinous instincts of those on display.

The Nags Head

Monmouth

Late in the evening.

Most revellers have headed away to seedier venues, but the gang has settled in another ancient, smoke-stained pub. No long counter in this one but a partitioned area that is divided around a horseshoe-shaped bar. The largest of these areas is home to a large, spitting fire nestled in a large, charred, stone fire place. Around the corner from this, a small nook is home to a loud and vociferous conversation.

At the bar, Graham, a packet of crisps clenched between his teeth, manhandles two handfuls of beer and short glasses off the tacky surface. He nods and grunts his gratitude to the barman as he turns toward the nook and the loud voices which spring from within. He steps toward, then rounds the corner heading for the small table where the gang sit. And another pretty girl, a 'Witch' this time, is draped happily over Ariff's shoulder; they huddle noisily.

As he approaches the table the front door to the pub is pushed open. Graham glances back to see Ariff's previous, paramour enter the pub. At the table the debate quietens as Graham shares out the drinks, eventually taking the crisps from his mouth to drop them in the middle of the table. Fast hands split the packet wide open and others begin to grab at this welcome snack.

Graham : (casually to Ariff) **Fairy's just come in.**

Ariff nods his acknowledgment to Graham and looks out toward the bar.

Brekk cannot disguise the glimmer of glee flashing across his features and turns to Tris at his side.

Brekk : (quietly) **He'll be in trouble now. If he had any brains this sort of thing wouldn't happen.**

He leans back and cranes his neck to look out into the bar area to see if this dejected sprite is heading their way. Graham retakes his seat, squeezing in amongst the others.

Jon : (Angry. Anger seems to be hard wired into his features, and with a mouthful of crisps, he restarts the conversation) **If Tris is allowed to believe in fucking Valhalla, then I'm allowed to believe in Heaven.**

Graham : (cynical) **But which Heaven?**

Jon : (fixing Graham with a strong look) **Proper Heaven.**

Graham : (ignoring Jon's intimidations) **Anyway, Tris doesn't really believe in Valhalla.**

Tris : (offended but expressed with a comical glance) **I do. I can believe in it If I want.**

Graham : **No you can't.**

Tris : **Yes I can.**

The others join in with a barrage of **'Yes he cans'** and **'He can if he wants'.**

Graham : (determined) **No he can't. Look, you can't *choose* to believe in something, you either believe it or you don't. You know, it's like, you don't believe television exists do you?**

Tris : **I believe telly exists!**

Graham : **Semantically, possibly, but in actuality you don't 'need' to believe it exlsts. You 'know' it does.**

Ariff : **So you don't need to believe it.** (Brekk shoots Ariff a quizzical glance) **If you know it.**

Graham gives a little nod.

Brekk : (still mildly concerned the fairy has not found Ariff with his arm around another girl, he decides to butt in, directing his observation toward Graham) **Of course, real belief can only exist in the *absence* of absolute knowledge**.

Graham : **Exactly, faith. But surely, the point of belief is that you do believe in the thing you have belief in. And you can't choose that.**

Ariff : **So anyone who says they believe in something, is really saying they don't 'actually' believe in it.**

Everyone looks confused.

Tris : **Well, I'm going to Valhalla and that's true because I believe it.** (Graham rolls his eyes) **Or, what's that one with all the virgins?**

Mac : **You wouldn't know what to do with a virgin.**

Ariff : **Ha, no, and they wouldn't know what to do with you..**

Jon : (to Tris) **Anyway Valhalla's for warriors isn't it?**

Tris : **Oh, is it?**

Mac : **You'll be alright; they'd need jesters too, I reckon...**

Jon : **Or someone to suck off the warriors.** (some wince in deference to the girl on Ariff's arm but she pays no attention)

Tris : **Wouldn't warrior types like buxom wenches doing that? Unless that's what you're into Jon, and there's nothing wrong with that.**

Jon : (not amused) **Fuck off...**

Graham : (looks to Brekk as the others continue) **What'd you get them started for?**

Brekk : (frustrated) **Well, I was trying to illustrate that this** (he gestures to the fancy-dress and Halloween paraphernalia adorning the pub walls) **is a representation of what is probably an early form of the religions that some think are still relevant.**

Graham shakes his head, not seeing the point of engaging this particular group's interest in such matters.

Jon : (angrily butting in to their side discussion) **Alright then, which one do you think is true?**

Brekk : **It's not really a case of which 'one', but where '*all*' those ideas came from.**

Jon : (warning) **You should be careful,** (he glances upwards) **you don't know who's listening.**

Graham : (raising his eyebrow in exasperation) **Exactly. And there are plenty to choose from.**

Brekk : **Yes,** (he stutters to get his point out before he loses their interest) **and, and many recycled, from earlier gods or religious figures. For instance, some of the earliest deities share the same historical details. Jesus, for instance, shares many of his experiences with the earlier Mithra and, even earlier than him, the Egyptian God Horus.** (he sees the others have started to pay attention) **Yes, all born to virgins, all dying for three days and being resurrected. All at the same time of year. It is widely, though quietly, accepted that these gods or religious figures are really just adaptations, personalized versions of a much earlier form of praise and exaltation. A more natural and ages-learned practice.**

Graham nods in agreement as the others look on in anticipation.

Brekk starts to relish the others in his thrall and pauses dramatically before…

Ariff : **Oh, um, Paganism ?**

Graham nods and the others coo at the revelation as John shrugs his indifference and Brekk shoots Ariff a fierce glance.

Mac : **Ooh, you clever fucker**. **You get a gold star for that.**

The 'witch' at Ariff's shoulder whispers something in his ear and everyone considers he's not just getting a gold star! Brekk's lip curls in disdain.

Tris : **Not just a pretty face, eh Ariff?**

Ariff : **Yeah I saw a program about it.**

Brekk : **I didn't think you'd read a book.**

Graham : (to Ariff) **Oh, when was that?**

Ariff : **Well, an advert for a programme, I dunno.**

Brekk : (trying to regain his control) **Whatever, Paganism is a broad term. But it isn't a single, encompassing philosophy or a 'religion', more a collection of ancient forms of trying to make sense of and worshiping nature and the natural workings of the world.**

Graham : (nodding in agreement) **Bizarrely, the genesis of both science and religion!**

The others are starting to lose interest again.

Graham : **But more pertinently, it's the reason the beer's half price and there are girls walking around with their tits hanging out.** (he nods at the buxom girl nestling against Ariff) **No offence.**

She smiles as the guys raise their glasses and release a small cheer in thanks to whatever has given cause to these welcome events.

Jon : (turns back to Brekk, angry and accusing) **So what makes your Pagan god more important than anybody else's?**

Brekk : **No, there is no Pagan god, well...that sort of came later. I mean they wouldn't even have called themselves Pagans. They weren't organised. Just inquisitive.**

Graham : **Inquisitive, but ignorant and creative.**

Brekk : (to Jon) **Pagans, well, you know, these 'Original Pagans', ended up worshiping the world and the seasons...**

Ariff : **Nature.**

Brekk : (shoots another stern look) **Yes, obviously. Nature. But their early, limited understandings and naiveties led them to give personalities and supernatural characteristics to the elements. And it's 'ironically' the evolution of those ideas which lead on, then, to the metaphysical and 'all-powerful' deities and, hence, religions, that are worshiped even still today.**

Jon looks angrily confused.

Graham : **Pagans, it would seem, were the first to 'believe'** (he does apostrophe fingers) **in 'magic',** (repeats the gesture) **which is basically what religious people went on to call their miracles. Trying to make sense or find reason for the stuff they don't understand, basically. What we now—when we have developed a thesis—call Science, really. When we understand it.**

Jon gruffly nods at this clarification. Then…

Jon : (starting sarcastically) **Well, if it is the first or 'true' religion then, why did it die out?**

Graham : (taking issue at Jon's misunderstanding) **That's not quite what he's saying...**

Brekk : **And It hasn't...**

Graham : (a confirming nod) **No, that's true; there are still plenty of people doing it. Practicing.**

Tris : **What? You're saying there are still witches about?**

Graham : **Technically, that would be correct.**

Mac : **Hey, don't they all dance about naked and stuff?**

Tris : **And there're all orgies and stuff like that.** (he smiles at Mac) **They love sex, the witches!**

Mac : (smiling and in collusion with Tris) **Oh yes. They love the sex.**

Brekk frowns his disappointment at this frivolous digression.

Ariff : (his lady friend whispering in his ear again) **Apparently you don't have to be a real witch for that to be the case. I think we're going to leave you to it.**

Brekk is slightly disturbed as he sees the 'fairy' walk past. She half glances into the nook but is distracted and moves on without a proper look. Ariff has his back to the entrance and she heads away, seemingly heading for the door.

Brekk : **Now** (then unusually loudly) **Ariff**, **Ariff, Ariff, um, hang on…** (everyone looks at him and he searches for something) **Um, uh, why don't we all go and find some real ones then?** (he still struggles) **Next weekend.** (thinking on his feet) **It's the proper Samhain, um, Halloween. If ever there was a time to find some practicing witches…**

They start to ponder this unenthusiastically.

Brekk : (again louder than is natural) **Ariff? What do you think?** (again too loudly, he sings it slightly) **Ariff? Or are you scared of the unknown? Eh, Ariff?**

Ariff looks slightly surprised by Brekk's directed tone but after a flash of consideration nods and smiles back to Brekk. Brekk beams back as someone turns into the nook.

Ariff : **No, never have been.** (He and his witch friend share a naughty glance). **Great, you lot sort out the details. I'll catch up with you in the week.**

His arm around his lady friend, he turns and nearly bumps into the 'fairy' who has returned to the entrance of the nook and found the elusive Ariff.

Brekk nudges Tris gently in the ribs as his eyes widen in anticipation.

Ariff, smiles as the fairy sidles up beside him and slips her arm around his waist alongside the other pretty girl's arm. She nestles her face into Ariff's neck while whispered words pass between them and then…the three of them straighten and head for the door. They half turn to nod their goodbyes and the girls give little waves. The guys around the table, slack-jawed, give little waves back. Brekk just looks dumbfounded.

Brekk : **Fucking hell, they're as daft as he is.**

They watch as Ariff and his two friends reach for the front door of the pub, pausing briefly as a couple of fresh faces enter. The entering patrons' faces light up as some recognize Ariff, and they spontaneously feel the need to shake his hand and give him a gruff hug. Some light banter passes before, Ariff and his pretty company leave, smiling.

The guys left at the table turn back to each other, their faces a mixture of respect, wonder, envy and, in Brekk's case, contempt.

Mac : (to Brekk) **Really, do you think there'd be witches, for real?**

Brekk : (bringing his confused ire under control) **Um, yes. In the right place at the right time, we could certainly be privy to some form of authentic witchcraft.**

Graham : (clarifying the point) **The fact that they're practicing the rituals doesn't make them 'real' witches. At least, not in the sense of real, 'magic' ones.**

Brekk : **Well, if we go somewhere with a proper lineage, who knows what we might find? What might be...**

Graham looks disappointed at Brekk's fanciful optimism and Brekk immediately regrets his words.

Tris : (turning gleeful) **That's beside the point isn't it? It's whether they need some willing participants to join them in their naked ceremonies.**

Jon : **Or just want fucking.**

Mac : (slightly surprised by Jon's frankness) **Quite.**

Brekk : **Yes, but to find someone with an understanding, a living link back to those early ideas. Who knows...** (he sees the others looking at him strangely before losing interest, he tempers his own.) **I suppose the only question, is where?**

Behind him on the wall, one of the homemade posters, advertising the evening's early Halloween event, is adorned with childish doodles. Among the scribbled zombies, witches, warlocks, bonfires and twisted churches which fill up the space on the paper, and amid the scruffy writing, a small doodle of a direction post, silhouetted against a full white moon, points away into the scrawled hills; along its length, scratched deep into the paper, the name Pendle rests in heavy graphite.

Pendle

The early sun shines brightly. Sunbeams, strong and sharp, cut through the fingers of the gnarled, wooden direction post, sculpting amorphous shadows within the soft lifting dew.

Carved into the wooden pointer, Pendle, it tells us, is 3.5 miles away. 3.5 miles along steaming, glistening roads, lined with golden, sunlight-tinged hedges and haloed trees.

The landscape breathes the rising mist in cold crisp gusts, which turn the fallen leaves and push and pull the long grasses, overgrown in the rusting fields.

In the distance, smoke rises from crooked chimneys as a rural community slowly comes to life. On the outskirts of the small village, toward some darkly wooded hills, a small but stately function hall bustles with chatter from within.

Once more a hooded figure struts, nervously now, across the stage. To his side, at the edge of the platform, two similarly cowled figures sit on old, plastic, chairs. The striding man stops, pulls back his hood and turns to address the gathering. It is the same man who addressed this same crowd not a week before.

Gilbert : (he looks pensive) **Our preparations continue well. The Master will be here in a few days and I'm sure we are all aware what an honour it will be to have him with us at this, 'The' most special, time.** (he looks across to the two seated figures) **You know, when the master came to the few of us a couple of years ago, he explained what a special and important place this was to him and how important and pleased he was that we were continuing the old craft. We had no idea then how progressive this movement could be. How powerful. I know the master has great plans for us all.** (another glance toward the 'hoods' is met with a slow encouraging nod) **It is with this in mind that I would ask you again to consider your level of commitment to the craft, and to the Master. It would be a great honour for us if we could help bring forward the Master's plans. It has been made clear to me that the rewards would be…unending.**

He strides across the stage once more, then lifts a hand and offers it toward the seated figures.

Gilbert : **These two…** (he's not sure of his next word but tries…) **Gentlemen?** (one of the figures nods noncommittally while the other merely shrugs) **have been sent by the master to help with our final preparations. We will do well to offer them our most fervent support.**

They stand but then do nothing except stare out at the crowd seated below.

Gilbert : (awkwardly) **Right.**

…

Across the brooding, verdant, undulant landscape and nestled within a small scattering of houses, is a small, crooked cottage, where an old lady shuffles through a narrow passageway, passing by a small reception counter and making her way toward the front door. She pulls the heavy door open and looks out on the glorious morning. Throwing a handful of seeds into the air she quietly mutters a few words.

She looks down the higgledy garden path where, at the forever open wooden gate, long past working and grown through with long grasses, a sign hangs on a wonky post. 'The Little Sister B and B'. The painted letters are worn and sun-bleached; underneath, hanging from a small wooden peg, another smaller, less tatty-looking sign suggests that there are, in fact, 'Vacancies'.

The old lady grunts at the sign, then turns back under the doorway.

Lilleth : (shouting as she shuffles back through the corridor) **Shem!** (no answer) **Shem!**

She moves down the ages-worn flagstones to a closed door on her right. She turns and pushes it open. A shawled figure sits at an old wooden table, a thin finger follows lines of letters and strange writings that fill the pages of an ancient-looking book which lies open in the centre of the table.

Lilleth : (shouting, short tempered) **Shem!**

The figure at the table turns slowly, wide eyed...

Lilleth : (immediately calmed) **Oh, it's you.**

...a young girl, twentyish, glasses propped at the end of her nose and eminently sensible by demeanour.

Cerrick : **Hi Lilly.**

Lilleth : **I could do with some help you know ? It appears we may be expecting guests!**

Cerrick : (without looking, she closes the book and drags it from the table) **Of course**.

As she gets to her feet, she slips the book into one of the wide pockets of her old, grey cardigan. She walks to the doorway and turns to edge past Lilleth who is slow to move out of her way.

Lilleth : (warmth and a smile in her voice) **When you are here, Cerrick, you should try to enjoy yourself. There's really no need to concern yourself with this business.**

Cerrick : (stops at the doorway next to Lilleth) **Shem is concerned.**

Lilleth : **Shem worries too much. Always has done.**

Cerrick : (a small smile) **I'll start upstairs.**

Cerrick ducks, needlessly, under the low door frame and heads away down the corridor. She glances back before heading up a twisting stair at the end of the hall.

Lilleth : (watching fondly) **Okay, my darling, okay.**

Lilleth starts slowly down the corridor until she reaches the small counter. She peers over the worktop to the wall beyond and a calendar that hangs, lopsided. As she scrutinizes the date and the notes, which are scrawled into the boxes marking the coming weekend, her eyes narrow in consternation.

The Van Friday 29th

It's pissing down and its dark. The sun has long since tucked itself behind a duvet of thick, grey cloud.

Standing in the rain is Brekk. An open umbrella wedged awkwardly under his arm, he holds a small tatty book at reading distance as he curls his other hand in strange movements and reads odd words aloud. This reading culminates in a flurry of dancing fingers as the passage comes to fruition and he glances to the ground where he has ended the incantation, pointing at a stick that lies near the curb. He stares at it with some anticipation. Nothing. He waits. He sighs and awkwardly turns a page.

Brekk : (reading from the book) **Essdamgrah! Essdamgrah!...** (he changes his tone and pronunciation and repeats, softening to a whisper) **esdumgrer...essdoomgrah...** (he is losing interest)

Brekk sighs and checks his watch. The small dials tell him not only is it Friday but that it is eighteen minutes past three o'clock.

He waits a little longer before pulling out his mobile phone to call one of the guys. It's answered quickly.

Brekk : **Where are you, you bastards?**

Mac : (from the phone) **Hey, alright Brekk. Haven't you talked to Ariff? I talked to Ariff; he should be there by now.**

Brekk : **What? Is he driving? I thought you were going to drive us. I'm still surprised he can coordinate any of his limbs. Well, other than his cock.**

The weak beams of light that struggle from the front of Ariff's van peek through the rain as he pulls around the corner into Brekk's view.

Brekk : **Oh, here he comes. Alright, I'll see you in a bit.**

Mac : **Yeah, see you later.**

Out of the grey, heavy rain, an old VW panel van chugs up as Brekk stuffs his phone and the book into the pocket of his heavy coat. Behind Ariff at the wheel, the front seats are partitioned from the back by a roller blind. The van stops and Brekk, at the window, sees the empty seats next to Ariff. He reaches for the back, side door. Ariff leans across and taps on the window, catches Brekk's eye and points to the empty seat to his side. Brekk sighs and opens the passenger door.

Ariff : **I didn't think you'd come.**

Brekk : (arrogant) **Well, it was my idea.**

Ariff : **Yeah, but I didn't think you'd come on your own without Mac.**

Brekk : (climbing into the van) **I don't need Mac to hold my hand, thank you...**

Ariff puts the van into gear and pulls off. The van stutters and he has to over-rev the engine to get it to play ball.

Brekk : (realizing what Ariff has just said) **What, he's not coming? I just spoke to him; he didn't say anything.**

Ariff : **Yeah, he called last night.**

Brekk : **Last night!**

Ariff : **Yep, he said him and Jon were off to his sister's Uni, some big party or summat. Sounded good; almost tempted myself.**

Brekk : **Oh, you were invited were you?**

Ariff : (a little confused) **No.**

Brekk : **Jon's not coming either?**

Ariff looks across at Brekk, then back to the road.

Brekk leans around and, with his finger, lifts the separating screen to peer under and into the back of the van.

Ariff glances across at him and smiles to himself.

Brekk : **What about the others?**

Ariff : **Don't worry, we're g..**

Brekk : (interrupting) **I'm not worried.**

Ariff : **... going to get them now**.

Brekk : (seeing a chance to clarify his position) **No, I don't need other people's affirmations. I don't need that constant reassurance of my worth.**

Ariff : (noting Brekk's unusual proclamation, he smiles) **Oh. Very good.**

The van swings around a greasy corner and trundles to the side of the road where it pulls up in a dark street outside a row of uninspired, terraced housing. The street lights above them blink, uninterested in anything other than inducing epilepsy.

They sit and wait.

Ariff looks across to Brekk who is insistently staring out of the window.

Waiting.

Ariff picks his phone off the dash to look at the time then puts it back down.

Ariff : **So, you know what we were talking about the other night, about belief and stuff.**

Brekk : (lets out a small groan) **Um, well there's a lot of issues, it's not really worth... Let's wait until the others get here.**

Ariff : (earnest) **I *am* interested, Brekk.**

Brekk : (turns slowly toward Ariff, then attempts his own earnestness) **No, that's good, and I'm interested in what you've got to say. It's just, you know, we don't want to exclude the others.**

He turns back to look out of the window and into the slashing rain.

On the dashboard Ariff's phone breaks the fresh silence as it starts to vibrate before the ring tone strikes up. A comedy ring tone, that sounds like a heralding fanfare which grinds to a faltering, computer glitch of a finale. Ariff laughs to himself; it gets him every time. Brekk visibly shudders as Ariff reaches for the phone.

Ariff : (into the phone) **Yeah, yeah...wicked, alright. Okay, yeah...yeah. Ha-ha, okay, cool buddy, wicked.**

He shuts the phone, slides it onto the dashboard and turns to Brekk.

Brekk : (grim faced) **They're not coming either are they?**

Ariff raises a little shrug of a smile before he revs the engine and the van pulls away from the curb. Brekk's expression sours.

Brekk : **Look, I don't mind if you don't think it's worth going.**

Ariff : **Eh? No no, that's alright.** (then really earnest) **Really, I'm as keen as you. Anyway, you were on about some party weren't you? All those witches dancing naked around their camp fires, looking for poor helpless lads to practice their spells on. I'm um,** (smiling broadly) **quite interested myself.**

Brekk : (condescending) **Oh no, it's not a party, it's not really like that at all, it's more of a cerebral thing. Look, it probably could have been fun if the others had come but I don't think you're going to enjoy the sort of thing I want to do. It's more of an intellectual exercise.**

Ariff : (enthusiastically) **Hey, really, that's fine, I like talking to people. I can do some, er, interviews, research, that sort of thing. I've always thought I could do with a more, er, intel,,,igentual way to spend my time.**

As Ariff talks, Brekk watches him as he listens, his expression growing more twisted as the horror of this inevitable union seems destined to be consummated.

Ariff : (seemingly oblivious to Brekk's dismay) **To be honest, I've always been interested in a lot of the things you talk about. I don't seem to get the chance to talk to you much. We can use this time to discuss stuff.**

Brekk : **Discuss stuff, excellent.**

The van turns through the puddled rural lanes. They sit in silence, other than the sound of the straining engine, as Brekk quietly dreads Ariff's next comments.

Brekk : (reaches for the radio) **Do you mind?**

Ariff : **No, no, go ahead.**

He turns the dial and a crackly noise fills the air. A little tuning and a local newscaster is discussing an upcoming election. Brekk settles back in his seat.

Ariff : (enthusiastically) **See, politics!** (Brekk's eyes widen) **I love politics.**

Brekk : (incredulous) **Really?**

Ariff : **Yeah, you know, all the, um, machinations and stuff.**

Brekk : **Machinations?**

Ariff : **Yeah, you know. This person disagreeing but that person not and then someone votes differently to how they should or something. Fascinating!**

Brekk : **Isn't it.**

Ariff : **But what I haven't worked out is, you know, what is the difference between, like, Conservatives and um, Labour. You know, that sort of thing.**

Brekk : (pained) **Sheesh, did you go to school?**

Ariff : (a little offended) **Well yeah, but they didn't really go into that.**

Brekk : **Um, look, I'm tired, I think I'm going to have a bit of a nap.**

Ariff smiles and nods his understanding as Brekk huddles down against the door at his side. Brekk's eyes stay wide and alert as he wonders exactly how bad an idea this is.

The van cuts its way through the foul squall, disappearing into the gloom.

To Pendle

In the blowing gale, Brekk stands against a hedge. He looks over his shoulder to see Ariff, who is pissing against the back wheel of the van. Even here, pissing amid the squall, he can't help but notice how effortlessly good-looking Ariff is, and a disdainful curl of his lip tightens his cheek. He turns back to his own, seemingly frustrated ablutions.

They have pulled over on a leafy rural lane. An archway of trees spanning the road, reaches away into the dark.

Amidst the gusting wind Brekk looks down to his own, uncooperative cock.

Brekk : **Come on, come on.**

The wind swirls, Brekk shrugs his jacket tighter when something, a noise in the air catches his attention, then, bizarrely, it seems to call his name. He turns toward Ariff.

Brekk : **What?**

But Ariff is paying him no concern. His eyes narrow in confusion; then, he hears his name called again. Whispered.

His attention directed, he lifts his ear. Alert now, he looks into the darkness beyond the trees. Again, there is a voice.

Voice : (still a whisper) **Brekk.............. Brekk........**

He peers deeper into the darkness, through the thicket...

Voice : (getting louder) **Brekk...**

He looks back over his shoulder and sees that Ariff does not seem to have heard the voice.

Voice : (losing patience) **Brekk!**

He peers, more determined, amongst the foliage and suddenly, there amid the scatter of greens and shadows, a pair of eyes seem to glow as they watch him. Brekk's breath catches in his chest.

A slender wrist and hand emerging from the hedge unfurls long, slim fingers and the delicate limb reaches out and takes Brekk's own eager hand. Brekk glances over his shoulder as he ducks into the wall of leaf and twig.

He cannot see who takes him through the flora but they glide, effortless, through the sticks and branches until…a clearing.

In wonder, Brekk looks upon the delicate, beautiful, naked woman who has led him and immediately starts to notice that behind her, in the darkness, highlighted by the moonlight, are more naked figures, lithe and oozing, pressing forward, toward him, their obvious desires reaching out to him.

Witch : **You have come to look for us?**

Brekk, dumbstruck, nods.

Another : **You wish to understand our ways?**

The 'witches' behind are moving together, wrapping themselves around one another.

Brekk : (eyes alive with wonder and desire) **Yes, yes. Please!**

Behind him in the distance another voice. It's Ariff.

Ariff : **Brekk!**

Witch : (she moves toward Brekk and places a hand on his belly, pushing her fingertips down past his belt and into his shorts) **And your friend, does he wish to know our ways?**

Brekk : (behind them Ariff calls again) **No, no he's not interested.**

Ariff : (closer now, pushing through the brush) **Brekk?**

Witch : (her hand pushes down, searching out his quickly stirring prick) **Are you sure? He has come with you to find us…**

The witches behind are now fully and lasciviously entwined, almost melting into each other.

Brekk : (frantic, excited and angry at the approaching Ariff) **No, he's really not the right sort of person……**

Ariff : (fighting through the bushes) **Brekk, come on!**

She grabs Brekk's cock.

Brekk : (Excited, angry, wide-eyed as Ariff bursts through the foliage and enters the clearing) **Ariff, fuck off!**

He sits upright, wide-eyed, jerked awake by his own vehemence. Ariff, still behind the wheel, looks at him with a little concern.

Ariff : **I thought we'd stop for a cuppa.**

Brekk blinks himself awake and aware.

Ariff : **Are you okay?**

Brekk : **Oh, fuck...** (reality crashes home) **Um, yeah, I'm fine,** (then sheepishly, while subtly adjusting his crotch) **sorry.**

Ariff has pulled into the car park of a busy service station, steering the van amidst a procession of graffiti-daubed vehicles and pedestrians whose garb would suggest their affiliation to some quasi-religious sect or group.

Brekk : (quietly disparaging) **Oh jees!**

They are walking through the happy group, Brekk sneering openly as Ariff smiles and nods at the overly polite, bustling people.

Ariff : **Not impressed?**

Brekk : **You can't just make stuff up.**

In the cafe they sit, drinks in hand, squeezing onto a long bench among the bustling and nattering group.

Ariff : **But I thought that was your point,** (he struggles a little putting a full thought together) **that all of the modern religions were made up, though, um, evolved from something older.**

Brekk : **Yes, but not on a whim. The passage of time might give gravitas to some that they don't deserve. These people no longer have ignorance as an excuse.**

Ariff : **But what if they're right? Surely their belief in whatever is as valid as anyone else's.**

Brekk : (sarcastically) **As valid, yes. Look, you said it yourself**.

Ariff : **I did?**

Brekk : **Yeah, 'Someone who says they believe in something is really saying they don't believe in it '. This,** (he gestures to the group around them) **this is just wishful thinking. They may indeed want, whatever it is they have chosen to believe in, to**

be true, but no matter how much they tell themselves, on a deeper level there is no real belief, a shallow delusion maybe.

Ariff is nodding some hellos to some of the smiling and circling congregation. Brekk can see that Ariff's warmth has made them ripe for approach. He raises his eyes in despair and stands.

Brekk : **Come on. How far away are we?**

Ariff : **Couple of hours still, I think.**

Brekk : **Let's get going. Before they try and make friends with us.**

Ariff : **Oh.** (he rises and follows Brekk as he nods commiseratory looks to the disappointed few who were optimistically approaching)

Outside, in the dark, rainswept carpark, the pair approach the van.

Brekk : (stopping at the van he finds a conclusion) **Real belief must be something more fundamental, a quiet understanding of the true nature of things.**

From behind Brekk, a voice.

Shadowy hooded figure : (soft, mellifluous tones) **It is discovering the true nature...**

Brekk jumps letting out a little screamy yell.

Behind him the hooded figure stands, two attendees at his shoulders.

Hooded figure (Devvin) : (reaching out to the vexed Brekk) **Sorry my friend, I'm sorry. Are you alright?**

Brekk : (catching his breath while recoiling from the offered aid) **Fucking hell!**

Devvin : **I'm sorry, I, we, were just passing and I heard your comment. About 'Belief. The true nature of things', and...**

Brekk : (interrupting, angry) **Well, don't creep up on people.**

Devvin : **I am very sorry my friend.** (Brekk is reaching for the van door) **Please allow me to get you something, from inside; I am here to talk to some other new friends about these very ideas.** (he gestures toward the cafe)

Ariff optimistically looks to Brekk, wondering if they will be accepting the offer.

Brekk : (exasperation) **No! Shit, we've just come from in there.**

And he cracks open the door and pulls himself up into the van. Ariff looks to the hooded figure and lifts his brow in a friendly apology, before climbing into his own seat.

Devvin : **No matter, and safe journey.** (He watches as Ariff starts the van and they prepare to leave) **Perhaps we will meet again and can discuss 'Belief and the true nature of things'.**

Inside the van Brekk pulls an obviously fake smile. His teeth glint under the lights.

Brekk : (under his breath while maintaining his rictus grin) **Fucking hope not, weirdo.**

Through the window Brekk watches the hooded figure as they pull away, chugging into the dark sodden night.

The hooded figure watches as the van dissolves into the rainy distance and out of the gloom the two hooded men step up behind him.

Hoodie2 : (a hiss hangs about his words) **We should go in. We don't have much time here.**

Devvin : **Yes, yes**. (From under his dark hood his eyes narrow as he watches the van disappear from sight)

He turns and starts toward the cafe building, the two hooded figures at his shoulders.

Devvin : **And which group is this?**

...

Back in the van.

Ariff : **He seemed nice...**

Brekk's face spasms in exasperation.

Brekk : **You think everybody's 'nice'.**

Ariff shrugs to himself while a smile of agreement wrinkles his features.

Brekk : **He looks to me like some narcissistic twat who's found himself in a position to exploit some vacuous, spiritually hungry teenagers. It'll all come down to sex and death.**

Ariff : **Eh?**

Brekk : **He'll be getting them to jump into bed with some made-up nonsense about preserving the soul past this realm and into the next. Being special, the chosen people, all that bollocks. All the time tweaking some insidious power structure to keep everyone in place.**

Ariff : **Isn't there a possibility he might be right?**

Brekk : **Bollocks, they're all the same. It's part of this new wave of bollocks and spiritual groups which are fucking everywhere at the moment. Its basic manipulation. You use everybody's natural fear of death and the unknown to manipulate and abuse them. Any,** (he fixes Ariff with a stare) **half-charming arsehole can take advantage, once they see how easy it is.**

Ariff : (concentrating on the road) **Not everyone's afraid of death.** (Brekk lifts a disbelieving eyebrow) **I'm not.**

Brekk : **Well, I think it's easier to say that than prove it.**

Ariff : **No, I might be concerned about the way I die, but not being dead.**

Brekk : **Oh, and why not?**

Ariff : **Well, we've all been dead before haven't we?**

Brekk : **Hmmn, reincarnation?**

Ariff : **No. Not alive before, dead before. You know, whatever it is that makes us 'us', well... when we die, it...** (he struggles to find the words) **um... disperses and returns to whatever it was before it came together, you know, before we were conceived. So, if that's 'dead' then it's just returning to a state we've already, um, been in.**

Brekk, despite himself, is a little impressed and narrows his eyes as he considers his response.

Brekk : **It's not an original idea, I suppose. Even that is a Pagan concept, the spirit *returning* to the earth.**

They drive on in silence for a while.

Ariff : **I hadn't realized you were so interested in all this... um..., religious and... Pagan stuff. You haven't talked about it much, before.**

Brekk : **Well, the others, they...** (he starts again) **No-one talks about it or takes it seriously...** (he looks across to check Ariff's reaction) **Not that I do, but... in an intellectual, you know, social history kind of discourse, it's quite an enlightening window into the psychology of the masses at differing times through an evolving society!**

Ariff : (looking somewhat confused) **Yeah, cool. So, you don't believe in witches and magic...not really?**

Brekk : **Well, witches are a fact. All across Europe, hundreds—maybe thousands—of women and men were murdered by the state for being witches. Only a few hundred years ago. People, even intelligent people like...** (he pauses) ...**um, me, believed—believed to their core—that there were witches: 'magic' witches. Believed it enough to kill people, burn them alive. Think about that. Then and now there are practitioners of that same ancient craft.**

Ariff : **Ok, witches, but magic of some sort?**

Brekk : **Hmmn. Well, there you are. That's not so clear.** (He thinks a moment) **You've heard of Voodoo, right?**

Ariff : (he nods) **But that is nonsense isn't it?**

Brekk : (vehement) **Absolutely not! The movie stuff, zombies and all that, of course. But there are documented cases of victims who, believing in the power of a curse, then succumbed to its poisonous effects.**

Ariff : (looking at him sceptically) **Really?**

Brekk : **Well of course.** (exasperation) **I can't believe how oblivious you, everyone is to this stuff.** (Ariff pulls a face) **I mean, you do have access to libraries or the internet; you do have interests I presume?**

A small sly smile curls Ariff's lip.

Ariff : **Well, yeah, I got a few....**

Brekk : (recognizing Ariffs flippancy he lets out a small grunt of disapproval) **Urgh, look. There was a very well publicized story about a pianist who was 'hexed' because of some insult or something. A witchdoctor cursed him publicly and it was reported on all the news and papers and everything. But although the pianist, deep down believed in the magic he couldn't openly say that, you know, in these 'enlightened' times, so he went ahead with his concert, which because of the interest was broadcast live, and halfway through the concert, just when the witchdoctor had said he would, small mistakes started to creep into the performance until after a cataclysmic mistake the pianist collapsed and has never played publicly since.** (he looks over to the wide-eyed Ariff) **Ok, so that shit's real, has real effect; however you want to explain it, that happened.**

Ariff : **Ok, but isn't that because he believed it?**

Brekk : **Well... yes, but that doesn't dismiss it's power. If the curse wasn't put in place then it wouldn't have happened. There's a million cases. When the victim believes, an idea planted by a witchdoctor or warlock or witch can lead to tangible, disabling fear. Creating hallucinations, paranoia and even death. Or similarly, the fulfilment of an incantation can affect the way things turn out...**

Ariff : **So you do believe in magic.**

Brekk : **Well,** (he considers a moment) **not like in the movies and stories and hocus pocus and all that, but a natural form of manipulating natural phenomena and nature and people, that is more understandable.**

Ariff : **Why would you want to manipulate people?**

Brekk : **It's not about manipulating people it's...**

Ariff : **Well, that's what you just said!**

Brekk : (angry at Ariffs interrogation) **Well what about you? You're 'Mr. popular'. It gives you a certain social standing.**

Ariff : **What?**

Brekk : **Well you know… the girls love you, guys love you...**

Ariff : **But that's not important!**

Brekk : **No, no it absolutely isn't! But it does happen to be the case.**

Ariff : **But that's not manipulation! I would say that I have a...** (again he struggles to find the words) **Tangible!** (very pleased with himself) ...**um... enjoyment in other people's happiness, their enjoyment! And as far as the girls are concerned, well that's just having fun. If there's a difference it's just that I'm not being dishonest.**

Brekk : **Dishonest!**

Ariff : **Well yeah, I'm always honest about what's going on. I don't pretend I want more than some fun. I know you and the boys always think everybody else is constantly shagging and everything but. Well yeah, sometimes there's shagging, but usually it's just having a laugh. I mean look at Jon.**

Brekk : **Well, he does alright.**

Ariff : **Does he? He lies to everybody. He lies to the one girl he says he loves most in the world and then he lies to his bit on the side. Jon, the 'real' Jon, whoever that is, doesn't actually exist in either of those girls' lives... It's like he needs to conquer women, he thinks he's some sort of 'James Bond', he's got a James Bond complex.** (Ariff widens his eyes, aware he has been clever) **Yeah.**

Brekk : **And what do you care?**

Ariff : (he finds his own exasperation) **I presume you do have a mother, maybe a sister, maybe one day a daughter...**

Brekk stops for a moment, caught up in thought. Several different concepts fight for prominence.

Brekk : (pensive) **But sometimes, when you're honest, well, some people don't find that attractive.**

Ariff : **Well, maybe you're just not trying, or not trying hard enough to...**

Brekk : (interrupting angrily) **Oh, so you admit you're 'trying'! Which suggests you don't mind projecting a false representation of yourself, which is different to Jon, how?**

Ariff : **Hang on, I think there's a difference between trying to be a decent, fun person and just trying to appear a decent one in order to fool someone into a shag. You're suggesting we shouldn't make any effort.**

Brekk softens his stare, tacitly conceding the point.

Ariff : **But anyway, if someone you approach doesn't want to know, why would you want to spend time with them anyway?**

Brekk : **A shag, I guess. But what about old-fashioned romance, determination...**

Ariff : **Stalking?**

They share a small smile while Brekk also shakes his head at the thought.

Ariff : **Anyway, you're probably as successful as me when it comes to women.**

Brekk : (disbelief) **Really?**

Ariff : **Well yeah. Out of every hundred or so girls I approach I probably only get between ten and fifteen, of what you might consider, 'positive' results. If that's how your judging things. And by the time you've approached ten girls I expect you'll be up to one or two positives yourself. So, you know, statistically...**

Brekk : (a natural smile gives way to a forced frown) **But look, this is my point. I think that your social gifts are, unwittingly perhaps, but they are an example of the manipulation of nature.**

Ariff looks at him, a little bewildered.

Brekk : **Look, when two people meet and don't get on, they might go on to say that they don't like each other, but that opinion is rarely based on a detailed analysis of the other person's character or morals. It's usually nothing more serious than a differing sense of humour or bad conversational timing.**
But someone who can control their initial repulsion to a um... person or situation which makes them uncomfortable,

to get past that initial negative feeling and then control and manipulate their own responses so that they can build a positive and valuable experience or even relationship, let alone the ability to make the other person meet them halfway. That is a true manipulation of nature and natural impulses, purely by the strength of mind.

Ariff : **Yeah, yeah. Of course, it's just being nice really.**

But Brekk is not listening.

Brekk : **So, is it not reasonable to believe that greater effects could be achieved when other factors or elements are used in conjunction with that control, or even used to enhance that control and power of the mind?**

Ariff looks across at Brekk, who is now fully self-absorbed.

Brekk : **And this is where Original pagan practice comes in. It's well known that certain diets affect physical, but also intellectual abilities. 'Placebos', like voodoo, have tangible physical effect. Tradition, Ceremony can enhance confidence, which in turn enhances the chance of success. There must be other ways, if not a million more ways, of altering, manipulating, 'natural' situations.**

Ariff : (concerned at Brekks vehemence) **Yeah, that's interesting...**

Brekk : **It's like during the natural disasters that have**

happened recently, the earthquakes and stuff, it's been well documented that animals have been distressed well before any manmade instruments had noticed what was happening. Many even deserting and running for the hills. They are still in tune with the language of nature. Man, mankind, would have been in tune until relatively recently himself. The animals don't have the distractions. The modern world, technology, unnatural methods have conspired to shield us from the organic powers that surround us. If we could reform the link to the natural. Find a teacher, someone who has not forsaken that knowledge.

He stares somewhat maniacally toward Ariff.

Brekk : **Imagine the power if you could rebuild that link. It would be like being one of only a handful of people who had access to the internet. Like a natural internet. The power of the world!**

Ariff : (quietly) **If that's what's important to you.**

Brekk : **Potions: what are modern medicines if not 'magic potions' by another name? Alchemy, the manipulation of the elements. Modern technology does it, our scientists evolved their educated understandings, but the ancients understood these principles before technology and education had proved to them the possibilities. They worked off of belief, natural belief. What the world has lost, Ariff, is 'True', 'Organic', belief, and the link to these powers along with it.**

Brekk goes quiet suddenly, a little embarrassed by his manner.

Ariff : (still surprised by Brekks vehemence) **So, you're saying this power, 'Magic', is real 'if' you believe in it.**

Brekk takes a breath.

Brekk : (he thinks) **No, it's not real *because* you believe in it. I mean, if it exists it exists. But maybe a natural, subconscious belief is part of the conditions necessary for it to work.**

Ariff : **But it's not like in the movies.**

Brekk : **I don't know. No, not 'Hocus Pocus', and stuff like that.**

Ariff : **So what is it like?**

Brekk : (quietly, still half embarrassed) **Well, that's what I'd like to find out.**

They share a serious look before both turn to stare out of the windscreen and they plough on into the dark, stormy weather ahead.

Amid the lashing rain the little grey van chugs away, further, until it is lost, once again, to the darkness.

Pendle

The B+B

Lilleth, cloth in hand, is busily knocking dust from the top of some of the pictures which hang throughout the hallway. A noise grabs her attention and she looks up toward the end of the hall. Shuffling backwards from behind the welcome desk, a tatty grey shawl stretches and sags as an old vacuum cleaner is dragged behind the counter and then into the hallway.

Lilleth : (mumbling to self) **Fuck it's never ending...Where does it come from?**

The figure turns and, to Lilleth's surprise, it is not Cerrick. A little wizened lady stares out from under the shawl.

Lilleth : **Oh. It's you.**

Shem : (she looks concerned) **Nothing is settled at the moment. I fear the fates are beginning to stir.**

Lilleth : **Now, don't get yourself all worked up. It isn't good for Cerrick; she is far too distracted by your worries. You know all is still vague at the moment.**

Shem : (takes her own book out of her pocket and looks at it with concern) **Yes it is, but if those vagaries that I have identified begin to condense then we will have been wise to be alert. It is hard to know how much to share.**

Lilleth : **Please be careful—she is at an age where she can be easily influenced or upset.**

Shem : (looking again at the book before stuffing it back into her pocket) **Yes lovely, yes.**

They share a glance of concern before slowly returning to their chores.

Arrival 9pm(ish)

The rain has recently stopped and everything glistens in the sharp moonlight. The departed storm rumbles angrily over the far horizon and distant bursts of lightening silhouette the destination amid the hills and woodlands of the dark and brooding landscape.

The van moves quietly along the shiny, puddled roads and Brekk and Ariff look to each other with some trepidation as they glide into an ancient village. The heavy slated roofs and crooked chimneys of the outlying, older houses slowly give way to a few more modern homes and buildings. Tarmac and cobbles lie side by side but give way quickly to more winding, country roads, leading to other antique villages and more meandering thoroughfares. Amid the old and new faces of the intermittently developed hamlets, Brekk and Ariff stare from the sparse comfort of the van, tacitly acknowledging that the need to find somewhere to stay is a priority.

They tootle about the wet streets and roads, eyes wide in hope. Down cobbled alleys, past graveyards and along country lanes. The streets are dotted with eerie-looking sculptures.

The sculptures, made of branches and twigs and adorned with scruffs of material, seem to appear at opportune moments, sometimes subtly, but others accompanied by a crash of distant thunder or flash of lightening, highlighting their surroundings and scorching the night sky. An air of desperation has gripped both Brekk and Ariff as they head the wrong way up one-way streets, realize they are going around in circles and fail to make sense of any of the seemingly randomly placed direction posts. All is in darkness; they are lost and, knowing it, are becoming distraught.

Brekk : (turning desperately in his seat to look back for clues) **Fuck! Fuck, fucking fuck!**

Ariff : (brightly) **Oh here we are. And there's rooms!**

Ariff pulls up alongside an old and crooked building. Light from several small windows light up a worn-out sign and a grassy open gateway. The Little Sister B+B. They nod to each other in shrugging collusion. Ariff puts the van back into gear and follows a gravelly pull-in, around the raised garden to a small yard, and the tires crunch to a halt over the loose chippings.

Brekk : (climbing out of the van, relieved) **I'll try and book us in. Get the bags and stuff**. (He grimaces as he looks around at the cottage and ramshackle surroundings, then at his watch) **We should be out already.**

Ariff : **No worries. I'm on it.**

Ariff circles round to the back of the van and pushes the keys into the lock on the back door.

As Brekk makes his way down the short path to the front door of the cottage, he hears from inside, a loud discussion; not wanting to intrude, he peers around the open doorway where he glimpses, at the end of the corridor, a girl. He notices how sensible she looks, a proud nose, and he considers her pretty, but is immediately taken aback by her loud and angry manner.

Cerrick : **No, *you* don't understand.**

He can't quite hear the responses from whoever the girl is talking to and he ducks away, trying not to be caught eavesdropping.

Cerrick : (still loud) **No, It must...** (she tempers her volume) **I'm sorry, but I must go tonight.**

Again, some muffled response which is obviously unwelcome and suddenly she is marching out. A startled Brekk takes a couple of steps backward to look as though he is approaching the door for the first time. He attempts to apply a fake, easy smile as he sees her nearing.

Again, another unwanted reply from inside and the girl's attitude redarkens as she nears the door. She turns back.

Cerrick : **No, I must have it tonight.**

She barges past Brekk as she exits the house.

Brekk : (turning to her with false confidence and forced smile) **Perhaps I could help out there...**

Without stopping she turns back, a little bemused but no less angry; their eyes meet, and she pauses.

Cerrick : **Fuck off !**

And she is away, out into the labyrinthine lanes.

Brekk looks out toward Ariff for some sort of confirmation of her fleeting presence, but Ariff is busy gathering stuff from the back of the van. Brekk, after peering into the darkness and, disappointingly, finding no trace of the girl, turns back and heads into the B+B.

Still a little shaken from the sharp rebuttal, Brekk steps up to the counter. He can hear some mumbling, punctuated with swear words. It seems to be coming from below the counter top. Brekk's eyes widen as the old lady, Lilleth, straightens from some business behind the work top to first scrutinise, then welcome him. She continues to scrutinise him despite his discomfort.

Lilleth : **Right**.

A short discussion and he is handed a key and pointed in the direction of the stairs. Lilleth watches him without a blink as he disappears up the stairs and she purses her lips in consternation.

Arms full, Ariff trails behind as they head up the stairs and find the numbered door. The heavy, ancient door creaks open to reveal a small room.

There is a large window at one end of the room above the head boards of two single, unmade beds which are pushed, with barely walking room between, against opposite walls. A small amount of standing room at the foot of the beds is next to a small built-in cupboard. Hanging, just barely, from a rusting bracket, sits an old heavy television, bearing a 'post it' note which demands 'Do Not Use'. A door opposite the window is wedged open and proves to be access to a tiny, tired, shower room. A plain 'white' toilet and simple basin with mirror above are crammed into the tiny space.

A pull chord which hangs beneath a yellowed fan is also labelled, again demanding, 'Do Not Use'.

Where possible the rooms have been clad in pine strip-wood, now darkly yellowed, and everywhere else a heavy plaster ridges collect thick dust.

Brekk runs his finger along a crease in the textured surface, looks at the dust on it with utter disgust. Ariff, seeing the look on Brekk's face, smiles to himself.

Ariff : (taking in the majesty of the room) **This is good, isn't it?**

Brekk looks at him, disgust still writ large across his features.

Ariff : (conceding) **Well, I guess it hasn't seen a lot of love since the seventies.**

Brekk : **The fifteen-seventies.**

Brekk smiles to himself, proud of his little joke as Ariff starts to empty his bag in a heap onto one of the beds and then starts repacking several items. Brekk watches, confused.

Ariff : (seeing Brekk's impatient interest) **Just packing some supplies.**

As if to illustrate he holds up the boxer shorts which are in his hand.

Brekk : **You're not planning on soiling yourself are you?**

Ariff : (chirpy) **Better safe.**

Brekk shakes his head and moves toward the door. Ariff grumbles at his own lack of preparation as he roots among his things before standing and grabbing the bedding rolled at the bottom of the bed.

Brekk : (angry impatience) **Time is finite, you know.**

Ariff : **Thought we'd make it comfortable for when we get back.**

Brekk glowers and Ariff, smiling, reassesses the priorities.

Downstairs at the welcome desk, Brekk quietly tries to get the attention of the old lady. Despite his attempts she rises slowly; pleasantly surprised to see him, she smiles a gummy grin.

Lilleth : **Oh, it's you again! Hello my dear.**

Brekk : **Ah, er, hello. Um. We're just off into town, and I was wondering if there was anything,** (he pauses, not sure of his wording) **anything, *unusual*** (he stresses the word) **going on, in town, this evening.**

Lilleth : **Oh, well** (turning back to the messy desk behind her) **I don't know I'm sure. Let's have a look.**

As she turns, Brekk is alarmed to see her long hook nose in profile, He watches intently as she scans the information on the cheap calendar pinned to the wall.

Lilleth : (cranes her head in an unusual motion back toward Brekk) **What do you mean by unusual, my dear?**

Brekk : (swallowing hard) **Um, well, you know, given the time of year and everything. Just, anything...unusual.**

Lilleth : (narrows her eyes) **Hmmm. Well...** (she turns back to the calendar and surrounding mess) **Bollocks. That bloody girl...** (she turns back to Brekk) **I wanted to go to this one.** (Brekk's eyes widen) **There is a gathering.**

Brekk : **Yes?**

Lilleth : (Again she scrutinises Brekk with cold detachment before...) **'The Old Chatterbox.'** (she sees he looks bemused) **The old public house in the middle of the village.**

Brekk : **Right.**

Ariff, alighting the bottom stair, nods hellos to both Brekk and the old lady and heads for the door. Brekk watches him leave while the old lady continues to peruse the calendar.

Brekk : **Will we be welcome?**

Lilleth : (she fixes him with a stern look) **If you're sincere dear. Now, shall I take your key, dearie?**

He holds the key up as he considers and like lightening her long spindly fingers are around his hand; then the other of her cold skeletal hands massages the key from his grip.

Lilleth : **You don't want to lose it.**

Brekk : (feeling disturbed and a little violated) **No, no.**

And he heads for the door.

Lilleth : **The front door's always open dearie.**

Brekk nods his understanding.

Lilleth : **The keyhole's a little rusty.**

Brekk : (under his breath) **I'll bet it is.**

Ariff is waiting as Brekk exits the B+B.

Ariff : (clapping his hands together) **Right, where are the witches?**

Brekk : (looking back toward the door) **Hmm?**

They turn away from the cottage and, taking deep breaths, both stare ahead along the glistening, meandering roads about Pendle. They start walking.

Ariff : **Any ideas?**

Brekk : **I think we should let intuition guide us. See if we can't get in tune with our own innate abilities.**

Ariff : (enthusiastic if a little bemused) **Cool.**

And off they head...

RE-BIRTHING CEREMONY
VILLAGE HALL
Friday 29th
9pm
FTW
ALL ESOTERICS WELCOME
Under Witch Hill

The Wizards Tipp

Brekk and Ariff amble through the small, twisting roads and streets. The tiny villages are nestled around the flanks of a brooding hill-scape. They march along the dark country roads between the villages and hamlets, looking for pubs or gatherings.

As they approach each hub of activity, Ariff, suggests they should explore, and each time, Brekk, remembering the name of the pub told to him by the old lady, dismisses Ariff's advice, telling him his own subconscious is not in accord and, under his insistence, on they go.

A period of frustration and Brekk is becoming agitated. They have arrived in a small village they have already passed through, at least once. They have walked a fair few miles and seem no closer to their quarry. Ariff, still buoyant, spurs them on and, on seeing some drunken revellers emerge from a tight alley they had previously missed, they head down a side street. A short walk until, before them, a modern pub. The Wizards Tipp.

Brekk : (angry) **No, No, No!**

Ariff : **Hang on. We can't be sure. We are, after all, trying to use skills you admit have not been...um...used, utilized recently. Why not give it a go? And to be honest, I really do have a strong feeling about this one.**

Brekk : **You've had a strong feeling about everywhere.**

Ariff : **No, this is different.**

Brekk : **Really. How?**

Ariff : **Um, well, you know. It's like the first time you're really in love, even though you thought you'd been in love before, you didn't know you hadn't been until the first time you realized you really were.**

Brekk : (considers) **No, I don't think that's it. I think it reinvents itself. So, you really are in love each time.**

Ariff : **Wow, I can't tell if that's more romantic or less.**

Brekk : **Doesn't matter. This isn't it.**

Ariff : **You seem very sure. I think it is!**

Brekk : (he looks to the sign above the door 'The Wizards Tipp' with derision) **Of course it's not it.**

Ariff : (quiet but firm) **Look, it doesn't matter if it isn't *the* place, it is a place, a place that sells booze! Let's just get some drinks while we still can. A freshener! and then we'll carry on. But, I really do think this is it.**

Brekk : **Alright, alright. if you want to waste time, and to prove, one way or another, the invalidity of your intuitive powers. A quick ale perhaps is in order. Lead on, Macduff.**

Ariff looks at him confused.

Brekk : **Fucking go in, then.**

And he offers Ariff the lead with a sweep of his arm.

Ariff opens the outside door and a wave of noise hits them. Brekk's face slumps in disappointment and he begrudgingly follows in Ariff's wake toward the busy bar. Brekk stalls as Ariff continues to the counter and he looks up to see, above the shiny modern bar front, an old wooden sign, now relegated to mere decoration. 'The Chatterbox'. Alongside are some black and white photographs which chart the renovation of the building. The few pictures show how fire had gutted the original, ancient pub. Brekk sees how the incredible age of the old sign is enhanced by charring and blistered paint. He looks to the bar and eyes Ariff with unusual scrutiny.

Ariff looks back from the bar to the now-approaching Brekk. He mimes with his hand drinking a pint and raises his brow to request Brekk's choice of beer. Brekk mouths 'Ale' as he approaches. He arrives at Ariff's shoulder as he is accepting the pints.

Brekk : (spotting jars behind the bar) **Ooh, I'll have a pickled egg as well, please. I'm starving.**

Ariff : (having placed the order he looks back to Brekk) **You do know, there is no known way of eating a pickled egg sexily, don't you?**

Brekk : **Not everything's about sex.**

Ariff doesn't look so sure.

Away from the bar now, they have found a little space amid the other drinkers. They take thirsty, welcome gulps as they eye the scenery, both decorative and human. Brekk tilts his head in preparation for his snack and lifts his pickled egg. But then, through the bar he sees them!

Through a couple of timber archways, in a side room off from the main bar is what looks, to all intents and purposes, like a 'coven' of witches, sitting around an old farmhouse dining table. Old women in shawls cackle and natter at each other. Across from the table an open fire is heating a boiling cauldron and at the side of the table the girl from the B+B sits among them. She is making notes in a small book she has open on the table.

As the pickled egg hits the back of Brekk's throat the girl looks up to stare straight at him.

With his head back and gullet open Brekk, realizing how ridiculous he must look, quickly turns his head away. He snaps his head forward and pours a large swig of ale on top of the unchewed, throat-nestled egg. Now, looking as normal as any other drinker swigging his pint, he looks across from the corner of his eye as the ale fizzes around the egg.

Ariff : **Hey, I think I'm right you know.** (he gestures toward the sign and some other information along one of the side walls) **This place used to be a house used by a local witch back in...**

Brekk's cheeks balloon under incredible force as he tries to incarcerate the increasing pressure but his eyes betray his impending surrender to the eruption at play within his mouth.

SPLAT.

Brekk, whose whole head seems to have swollen, makes a gulping fizzing regurgitation square in Ariff's face...

Ariff : (in a shocked falsetto) **Fifteen ninety-three!**

Ariff is stunned. Egg and ale drip down his face as from Brekk's, disbelieving, slack, sputtering mouth.

Ariff : **Fucking hell!**

Brekk : (shuffling Ariff off to one side, trying to compose himself) **Sorry, sorry. Shit...sorry**.

Brekk looks back toward the arches.

Brekk : (whispering loudly) **Over there, that's it, that's the coven meeting.**

Brekk, spying now, ducks down behind a wooden post as Ariff pulls a t-shirt from the backpack, He looks to Brekk and waves the T-shirt at him to illustrate his motive. Still in shock, he ambles off toward the loos, dripping ale and egg as he goes.

Brekk, bent over, continues to spy. As he peeks from behind the post an old bar towel presents itself and he casually uses it to wipe his face.

Ariff enters the gents as behind him, Brekk, now upright, is remonstrating with a young female drinker.

Brekk : **It might well be, but it does look like an old bar towel.**

In the loos Ariff is washing his face in the sink. He switches T-shirts, rinses, and after wringing out the soiled garment he moves across to the hand drier. He laughs aloud at some particularly unsavoury graffiti before his gaze alights on something of interest and he reaches up and tears it from the wall.

Back in the bar and Brekk is still angrily apologizing to the unaccepting girl. As Ariff steps up he gives the girl a huge confident smile.

Ariff : **Sorry, is he bothering you?**

He thrusts the crumpled paper into Brekk's hand and steps between him and the girl who has instantly reciprocated his warmth.

In Brekk's hand the small poster declares that, this very night, is 'A rebirthing ceremony, at the old ceremonial hall, under Witch Hill'. Further down the black paper it explains, 'All Esoterics welcome' and he looks up toward Ariff, who is swapping numbers and getting directions from his new acquaintance.

Brekk and Ariff are leaving the pub.

Brekk : **But what about what's going on in there?**

Ariff points to a large chalk board where, writ large is the message, 'Cooking Ye Olde Fashioned Way. Friday Eve'.

As they step through the door Ariff turns to be met with sad-faced waves goodbye from the girl and her friends at the bar.

The Daughters of Pendle

A long dark walk through and then out of the village finds them approaching a tatty corrugated hall with a few scruffy attendees milling about outside. The music gets louder as they near and Brekk is starting to throw concerned glances toward the happy and decidedly unconcerned Ariff.

Brekk : **This can't be it.**

Ariff : (his eye caught by some attractive revellers entering the building) **Well, we should at least have a look.**

Brekk, seeing some pagan symbolism and daubing around the building, concedes a brief recce is in order.

The music, unbearably loud, envelops them at the unmanned door and Brekk flinches as they enter.

Inside now, they circle the busy room and Brekk's fears are confirmed.
The event, although couched in the paraphernalia of the esoteric, seems to be nothing more than an excuse for a loud rave. He pushes, miserably, through the waves of idiots and notices a couple of hooded magicians on a small staging. They are engaged in some dark trickery and Brekk stops to see what childish misdirection they are employing to befuddle the cooing onlookers. Frustratingly, Brekk can't work out the misdirection behind the illusion, which only adds to his angry frustrations. He dismisses it and calls back over his shoulder.

Brekk : (shouting) **We should leave. We're wasting time.**

He manages to turn amongst the throng and is frustrated to see Ariff is no longer at his shoulder. Through the gaggle of drinkers and dancers he can see Ariff on the dance floor, already happily throwing shapes with fevered abandon, subsumed by a circle of encouraging girls and laughing, happy guys.

Brekk : (sheer frustration) **Motherfuckaagh!**

He forces his way through the mob and heads away, back toward the door. At the doorway he turns back to peer once more at the stage act. He concentrates on a now levitating ball of light, wincing in continued frustration as he tries to work out the form of deceit. His brow furrows in deeper frustration and he lets out a burst of angered impatience.

Brekk : **Pah!!**

Fidgety and angry, he bursts from the entrance and marches off down the road. Suddenly there is a voice behind him.

Ariff : (shouting) **Brekk, where are you going?**

Brekk : (turning, angrily) **This is not why we've come here.**

Ariff : **No, these guys are good. They're into all the, um, Pagan stuff and everything.**

Brekk : (Sarcasm doesn't quite cover it) **Oh really. Great, I tell you what, you carry on with your, 'Research and Interviews' here. See what you can find out about the 'Pagan stuff and everything'! I'm fucking going fucking back to the fucking pub!**

He turns, determined, and heads off into the darkness.

Ariff : **Oh, Okay.** (he watches as Brekk sulks away, then calls out optimistically) **I'll call you later. We can meet up before heading back to the B+B.**

Brekk : (A dismissive growl) **Whatever.**

Ariff turns. Then, after a small pensive glance toward the nearly out of site Brekk, he shrugs and, smiling, re-enters the deafening hall. The same group of girls and guys within let out a small cheer and beckon him back into their frenetic dancing mob. The door swings closed behind him.

...

The door to The Wizards Tipp swings closed behind Brekk as he stands in the doorway, a pained frown taking hold of his features as he, once again, contemplates the busy bar. He starts to push through the crowd and glances through the arches to see the old ladies still cackling around their table. Cerrick sits, fidgeting impatiently, among them.

As he pushes toward the bar a girl turns to see him, glances behind him and asks where Ariff is.

Brekk : **Oh, he had to go home, he had a terrible bout of the shits**.

Girl : **Really?**

Brekk : **Yeah, terrible mess.** (seeing the look on her face) **I'll ring him, tell him you're asking, though.**

Girl : **Um, no, it's alright, I'm busy anyway.** (she turns back to her friends)

Brekk : **Oh, ok.**

A sly grin and he moves on through to the bar. As he tries to order a drink he keeps peering through to the 'coven'.

Between the milling drinkers he can see that the younger girl, Cerrick, now seems to be quite vocal within the group while the other, much older ladies, seem to be trying to placate her.

Drink now in hand, he slowly makes his way through the drinkers and then beneath the arches that separate him from the old ladies and nestles himself behind a pillar, barely able, but trying to eavesdrop on their conversation.

He glances nonchalantly across the busy pub, then quickly looks back over his shoulder into the meeting room, trying to glean some information before quickly turning back to the pub and casually sipping at his beer.

In the small room one of the older women is trying to calm Cerrick's unheard concerns.

Rayshee : **...they are playing at the 'Old Craft'. There is no reason to give them any thought.**

Shar : **It's true, these children have neither the history or experience to engage with the Miasma, if they even believe in such a thing**.

Jeska : **Indeed, you should care as much about your studies, Crone.**

Some of the others cast disapproving glances.

Cerrick : (softly pleading) **Please don't call me that.**

Mysty : (addressing the whole table) **It is just her age. Weren't we all distracted by the thought of bigger, more important, exciting things conspiring against us from the shadows? More fun than this stuff.** (she prods at some of the papers strewn across the table and a few of the wrinkled gang burst into loud shrill laughter)

Behind his pillar Brekk recoils from the bone-rattling cackle.

Jeska : (sharply) **Don't patronise her. The sooner she grows out of this fanciful nonsense the better. There are real, if less exciting lessons to be learned.**

Ro'see : (loudly) **Who are you to tell her it's fanciful nonsense**?

Jeska : (contained anger) **Please. That's enough distractions. Without the foundations nothing of worth can be accomplished**.

The table mumbles its agreement.

Leanda : (quietly to Cerrick) **Sounds boring doesn't it?**

At the pillar, Brekk peeks around the corner to see Cerrick slump a little in frustration. He ducks back quickly.

At the table one of the wrinkled old women coughs a little to arrest everyone else's attention. Successful, she nods toward the arch at the far end of the room.

Brekk, again, casually peruses the bar and its customers then takes a sip of his drink and slowly turns his attention back toward the mostly aged group. He swallows hard as all at the table stare back at him.

Brekk : (shakily) **Hello!**

...

...

Strobe lights. Bruising rhythm.

Ariff is amid the writhing mass on the dance floor and, due to the loud thumping music, is having a shouted conversation with one of the beautiful girls who have taken him into their gang. She points at his shirt and the pattern scrawled across it. Some of the guys smile to each other as they distribute more shot glasses among their friends and all seem pleased to have Ariff in their midst. The music abates to the sound of chinking glasses and the group huddles chaotically around Ariff; he easily enjoys the affections of his new-found friends. Then, fresh beats pierce the momentary quiet and the whole group erupts in a glorious fountain of hair, arms and sweat as the next thumping sound explodes into the ether.

...

Brekk, wide-eyed, sits at the table among the old ladies and all quietly consider the uncomfortable looking young man before them.

George : (leans forward to begin her suspicious interrogation) **So, is it cooking you're interested in young fella, or is there...** (she glances across to Cerrick) **something else?**

A few of the others burst into their shrill cackle.

Brekk : (He looks awkward and coyly at Cerrick) **Oh god, no.**

Cerrick looks dumbfounded by this peculiarly determined response.

Brekk : (pained) **No, no… I mean… Its um, just, I'm fascinated in the way you, um, use your,** (he looks at the old papers strewn across the table) **ingredients and recipes.**

The ladies look to each other in short quizzical glances. A few start to mumble.

Brekk : (Quickly, he tries to stall their distraction) **I think it's interesting that the modern world is starting to look back at the ways our ancestors used to do things, you know, in trying to find solutions to modern problems.** (they start to take notice) **Natural, organic. Homegrown. All of these things are now thought of highly by growing numbers of people in our, um, society, uh… and cooks and that…**

Nods bounce around the table.

Ro'see : **Well that's right, of course.**

Rayshee : **Not enough people.**

A carafe that has sat in the middle of the table is suddenly passed his way and bony hands pour and shove the goblet in front of him.

Brekk : **Oh, er, thank you.** (He politely takes a drink, which feels like it strips the skin from the back of his throat. He coughs as the old ladies laugh) **cough** (He regains his composure and continues nervously) **I wonder, um, sometimes, um, what else society may have lost along with its disconnection from the natural world.**

He sees them eye each other suspiciously.

Brekk : (seeing they have not dismissed him, continues) **And I wondered if there wasn't more that these old recipes, ingredients and** (he takes a chance) **um, preparations may have to offer.**

George : (again through narrowed suspicious eyes) **Preparations?**

Armandle : (cutting to the quick) **Is it magic you're interested in?**

They lean in accusingly.

Shar : **Witchcraft.**

Mysty : **Spells and potions!**

Leanda : **Broomsticks!**

The cackle rises like a wave from the table and Brekk recoils in his seat. He looks deflated as they continue to tease him. He looks toward Cerrick hoping to find a supportive face but Cerrick is distracted, looking toward a large candle on the window sill. The candle's length is marked with numbers and lines, Brekk surmises it is a time piece.

Jeska : **I think you might be better off with the young-uns up on the hill.**

Cerrick : (snapping back to the conversation) **No...**

Brekk : **Oh, I've been up there. It's just a party. Loud and music...**

Jeska : (proudly) **There, what did I tell you. Children.** (she reaches for Brekk's goblet and throws the contents into a bucket that sits under the table then reaches for another carafe) **Here, try this one. It's not as rough. Leanda made that one. God knows what she does to it!** (she refills his cup)

Cerrick shoots Brekk an accusing stare which makes him shift awkwardly in his seat. Brekk takes a gulp of the new drink to distract himself from Cerrick's animosity. It is as rough.

Cerrick : (angry) **You should stay quiet about things of which you know nothing.**

Brekk, trying to ignore Cerrick's ire, coughs as this even fouler liquid hits the back of his throat.

Jeska : **A bit smoother?**

Brekk tries to disguise his grimace.

Angeline : **Now, now.** (addressing the still-rowdy table) **Settle, settle.** (she waits while the ladies quiet) **It would be remiss to ignore our young friend's, not unique, misunderstanding.**

The ladies have started to look to each other in a conspiratorial manner. Then they relax and their collective demeanour softens.

Armandle : (to Brekk) **What is, 'The question'? What is it that you really want to know?**

Brekk : (he looks around at the open, welcome faces and his mind fills with questions) **Um...** (the weight of their anticipation presses upon him) **um...** (his thoughts dissolve before their expectation) **Um...**

The ladies start to look to each other, and he feels their growing impatience.

Brekk : **Um...** (Armandle nods encouragement) **Um, is it, possible, for anybody to become a witch?**

A collective groan rattles around the table.

Ray'shee : **Well, that's not the bloody question is it?**

Angeline : **No,** (looks sternly at Brekk) **that is not the bloody question.**

Shar : **'Is there really magic?'. *That's* the question.**

Mysty : (to Brekk) **Isn't that what you really want to know?**

Brekk : **Yes, yes. Yes, it is, of course. Please.**

George : **I mean, what is a bloody witch? Someone who uses magic. If there is no magic, then there is no witches.**

Brekk, wide eyed, nods along to the line of logic.

Brekk : **And you are witches?**

The cackle is unleashed once more.

Ro'see : **Oh, darlin. Bless you. It is Samhain, Halloween, you know.**

Shassa : **We don't always dress like this, dearie.**

The cackle continues around the table and Brekk seems to shrink in his seat as the humiliation confines him. He takes another gulp of the fiery liquid.

Ary : **Oh dear, oh dear..**

...

The heavy rhythms continue as Ariff and another of the girls are getting close. The rest of the gang are still milling around their new-found friend but appear to be preparing to move on. On the stage behind them the two cowled magicians continue their tricks to a small appreciative part of the gathering.

Ariff : (glimpsing the magicians from the corner of his eye and quickly bewitched by the illusion) . **They're good, aren't they?**

Honey : (matter of fact) **It's all real, Ariff.** (her hand draws out shapes in the air in front of Ariff who seems relaxed in his acceptance as she hollers above the noise) **I can show you some more magic, more real magic. But we have to go on, there's another gathering. Just for the special people.**

She runs her hand over Ariff's muscled shoulder and she watches as her fingers sculpt his torso through his shirt.

Ariff : (also shouting over the music) **That's cool.**

Ariff pulls his phone from his pocket and waves it in front of her face. She nods her understanding as Ariff moves away through the gang and spies out the exit door. As he wriggles through the masses a shot glass is thrust in front of him and he stalls in his tracks and, smiling, accepts the glass. More cheers and more music and more alcohol.

...

The conversation around the table in the Wizards Tipp has settled and a more controlled discussion is taking place.

Shar : **I'm sorry, Brekk. You must understand we get a lot of people down here who have seen too many television programs about witches and magic. We like to have our fun.**

Brekk : (deflated but remaining polite) **Yes, of course. I'm sorry, I've fallen under the same misapprehensions as everyone else, it would seem. It's just such a compelling idea that a strong link to nature could yield some 'extra' reward.**

Ro'see : **Oh, It does, sweety. It does. It's just got nothing to do with broomsticks and warty old women.**

Brekk : **But why does this idea, this misconception survive?** (his goblet is nudged toward him once more and he reluctantly takes another painful sip) **There must have been something. More than just myth.**

Jeska : **Media bollocks. Romanticism** (trying to build import) **But, it has to be said, in the distant past,** (she gives Ro'see a glare of reprimand) **it is said that there was a power.**

Cerrick : (excited) **The Miasma**.

Brekk : (coughing his drink back into his goblet) **The Miasma?** (Gentle nods from many at the table) **But, well, that means, and I don't mean to be disrespectful, but 'Miasma', means a stinking foul putrid mess… Doesn't it?**

Mysty **: Well, it didn't used to!**

Jeska : (seething, quietly to herself) **They steal what they can use and twist and hide the truth by force of their message.**

A rumble of expletives jump from all around the table as Brekk nods his understanding.

Brekk looks back to Jeska, wide-eyed.

Jeska : **Yes, yes. But the key to that power, *'if'* it existed, has become lost, disseminated. First science, proofs and reason.**

And now certain kinds of technology, we believe, have disturbed the flow of the energies. And a shallow understanding of this new science has changed the way people believe...It has been lost to us and we must find another way forward. You, we all, must accept this.

Cerrick frowns.

Brekk : **Technology ?**

Jeska : **Radio waves and the like** (she wiggles her fingers in the air mimicking the phenomena). **The last nail in the coffin. As far as the old ways are concerned.**

Ary : (wearily) **Out here at least**.

Jeska : (shooting Ary a stern look) **Yes, we think the technology seems to have doomed the old craft.**

Brekk : (politely ignoring the stern look, an empathetic nod) **Of course. I suppose it's a double-edged sword. It's both a disruption and a distraction. People today, they don't seem to be able to move unless they've got their little personal device strapped to their ear.** (Most of the old ladies nod along with his concerns; he looks over to Cerrick to see if he has her attention but she is once again distracted by the timepiece on the window sill. Hiding his disappointment, he continues) **And it's all rubbish, if they're not watching pop idiots and telly idiots then they're talking about idiots or, worst of all, wanting to be idiots. So unnecessary. Too lazy to walk to a phone…or a library...It stilts thought and consideration...**

As Brekk waxes about his distaste, not only for technology but also the idiots who use it, a noise starts to quietly emanate from under the table, somewhere in the region of Brekk's pocket. It gets louder quite quickly.

Brekk : (realising his phone is ringing, his impassioned speech starts to falter)...**Um...**

Mysty : **Hadn't you better get that sweetheart?**

Brekk : **Um...Its um,** (He's already shaking his head as he pulls the phone from his pocket and sees Ariff's name pulsing on the screen and tuts his displeasure. Then, remembering where he is...) **It's not even mine** (he lies. He looks around for any generous faces) **I'll turn it off. Nonsense.**

He presses down hard on the off button and his phone dies a quick tonal death as he pushes it distastefully back into his pocket. Shamefaced but attempting nonchalance, he looks back about the group.

The old ladies look to each other in amusement.

Mysty : (generously) **I'm sure if we were your age we would all succumb to the same distractions you have to contend with. It is always a different world for the next generation. And we don't forge the world we are born into. Some of the older generations forget that.**

Brekk manages a small thankful nod at her understanding.

Cerrick starts to gather some of the papers off the table and, straightening them, places the pile into a small leather satchel that sits beside her on the bench.

Rayshee : **You going somewhere?**

Cerrick : **Well 'I'm' not learning much here. With all these distractions** (she shoots Brekk a look of derision as he pours himself another drink) **I'll be better off looking through these at home.**

Jeska : (suspicious) **Really?** (Cerrick's features turn guilty) **You're going home?**

Cerrick : **Yes.**

She turns quickly and takes a step from the table.

Jeska : **Don't forget your book, crone.**

Cerrick turns and without lifting her gaze grabs her small book. She marches toward the door at the back of the room.

Rayshee : (her eyes narrow) **Say hello to Shem for me!**

The room fills with the shrill cackle once more as Cerrick grabs angrily at the door handle and is gone, leaving the door rattling and swinging in the gale behind her. Brekk looks around at the shrieking old women and then his gaze alights on the slamming door. He gets to his feet and crosses to the exit. He reaches for the handle of the wildly swinging door and grips it firmly.

Before pulling it closed, he looks out into the darkness. The back of the pub. A small courtyard, ramshackle wooden panelling and gateways on each side. However, a small picket gate opposite the doorway swings loose and he tries to peer into the distance behind it. The darkness consumes the view, but Brekk sees that the pathway leads away between the gardens of old terraced houses before all is flattened into the blackness of the silhouetted hills in the distance.

George : (as the cackling abates) **Come back in, sweetheart.**

Brekk turns, disguising his interest, and edges back onto his seat at the corner of the table.

Shar : (raising her brow toward Brekk, requesting his interrogation) **Anything?**

Brekk : **Um, oh yes, of course. The Miasma?**

Rayshee : (sternly) **We must forget The Miasma. Its place is lost to history.**

Brekk : (a little deflated) **So there really is no Magic. No,** (he lifts his fingers and punctuates...) **'supernatural' abilities?**

Little comiseratory glances are rolled his way.

Ro'see : **Not like in the old days.**

Jeska : **Now we must accept that the only true magic is that of kindness.**

Ary : **Generosity, empathy. effort.**

Brekk curls his lip in distaste while glugging at the brew.

Armandle : **Psychological manipulations. To enhance confidence** (the others nod in unison) **and engage the subconscious**.

Mysty : **Yes. To enable positive results, then learning and knowledge, honesty, mindful experience. These are the skills you must master to change your path. There is no greater magic than that.**

Brekk : (impatiently dismissing this hippy bollocks) **But what were the parameters the limits of the old magic? This Miasma!**

Once again, the old ladies look to each other before a consensual shrug elicits more frank responses.

Armandle : **In times past, this area became known as a centre for witchcraft, as we know you are aware, but the practice continued long past the trials of the sixteenth century. The practice was passed from generation to generation until the last practitioners...**

Ro'see : (respectful) **The Daughters...**

Armandle : **Yes, The Daughters. But they, on realizing the dwindling potency of the Miasma, destroyed their texts and disbanded their affiliation. They knew that the world needed a fresh understanding. They took the fundamentals of the practice and designed a new message that would help the world survive the onslaught of global rationalism.**

Brekk : **You're saying the Renaissance, science and education are a bad thing.**

Jeska : **Well they are for witchcraft, for magic, for the right kind of belief. Isn't that what we're talking about? But the tenets of the practice...**

Some of the others start, then all join in.

All : **Respect for the world, respect for other people, respect for yourself.**

Brekk can hardly disguise his distaste.

Jeska : **They still form the basis of this new movement. Of course, we still use tradition and ceremony to commune with nature and use the natural world to remind ourselves and invigour our resolve. We would hope to set a worthy example.**

Brekk : (still full of distaste) **So you've just become preachers and teachers?**

Shar : (slight disgust) **Oh no. Examples, examples of a different way.**

George : (very intense) **Beware the teacher desperately looking for a pupil.**

Brekk : (barely hiding his impatience) **But what of the old magic? what could it do?**

Rayshee : (her own angry impatience erupting) **Obsessed, obsessed. We have told you the old magic is dead**. (somebody : *If it ever existed*!) **We expend our time explaining to you something relevant and worthwhile and yet you have no interest.**

Brekk : (contrite) **I'm sorry. And I am interested, but I think I already understand the new forms of practice you talk about, but also, I don't have a lot of time and when I came here, I was trying to research what turns out to be what you have called the 'old form of practice', 'the Miasma'. And I mean no disrespect but If you will grant me, I had wondered on the...**

(he's trying not to say power) **extent of the transformations and privileges it could manifest.**

Jeska : (disgusted at the idea) **No, not privilege. The Miasma was a powerful resource and capable, when understood properly, of most of your story book notions.**

Brekk : (wide eyed now) **Really.**

Jeska : (she nods sincerely) **But not privilege. Those powers of the Miasma which could be abused were rendered infeasible.**

Rayshee : **The power could not be used to aid oneself without either consultation or wage.**

Brekk : **Wage?**

Mysty : (answering Brekks question) **Sacrifice. Willing and honest.**

Brekk nods his understanding.

Rayshee : (Slamming her hand down on the table) **Enough.** (Abrupt and final) **We have wasted enough time on that dead craft.**

Brekk's frustration at his curtailed investigation flashes across his features.

...

Ariff walks among the tight, exuberant huddle along pitch-black country lanes into the unknown. He is still talking to the same girl. They giggle conspiratorially.

Honey : (grabbing Ariffs forearm) **You're perfect.**

Ariff : **You're not so bad yourself.**

Honey : (she smiles) **Come with me.**

Ariff complies happily, and they edge away, ahead of the rest of the group who nod to each other in excited, knowing collusion.

...

Brekk : (Standing, he drains his goblet and thrusts it onto the table then strides toward the doorway and opens the door) **Thank you, ladies but** (hiccup) **I must go.**

Ary : **Just remember the important stuff we have told you. If you want to change your life. The lives of people you love.**

Mysty : **That is the real magic.**

Jeska : **The only magic.**

Brekk : (still feigning interest but looking out into the darkness) **Yep…right.**

His eye is drawn to the slamming, wind-blown gate opposite the doorway and he squints into the blackness beyond.

Behind him the old ladies still beseech his interest.

Shar : **Respect for the world.**

Ro'see : **Respect for other people.**

Mysty : **Respect for yourself.**

Brekk : (he turns back) **Okay then.. Yeah, sure will. Cheers.**

He pulls the door closed as he steps into the gale, nodding his false affirmations as he goes.

Inside, the old ladies quieten quickly and look to each other, then all look to Jeska. She lets out a little sigh and a disheartened shrug.

Over Witch hill

Brekk stands in the tatty courtyard, dart-like rain slashing against his face. He pulls his jacket tight about him and takes a couple of steps toward the small, swinging gate. He squints into the darkness, looks about for some direction. Resolve evades him and he calls out.

Brekk : **Hello?**

He stares into the darkness.

Brekk : **Are you there?** (hiccup)

No response. He looks around, again waiting for some confident impulse.

A small guttural growl of frustration and he finds his purpose. He marches through the gate and into the darkness of the poorly lit pathway. A couple of ancient streetlamps barely light up dim patches further down the overgrown back alley and he wades through until, at the far end, past the houses, a rusted gate hangs open and a roughly tarmacked access area glistens in the wetted moonlight.

Other than following the rough tarmac around the end of the terrace to the main road, a wooden stile between rough hedgerows is his only waymark. He looks around before crossing the hard surface which falls short of the wooden stile and hedge. The soft mud he steps into gives way and cold water soaks into his sock and shoe.

Brekk : **Fuck, fucking fuck...**

He jumps from the puddle toward longer grass and the stile. Looking around at the dark panorama in front of him, his face is a picture of despondency.

Brekk : **What the fuck am I doing?** (hiccup)

He looks down to his sodden feet, then back toward the dimly lit pathway that leads back to the pub, the village. He hiccups again.

As he ponders his next move the rain stops and the moon reveals its bright, crescent self. In the brighter moonlight he sees fresh muddy smears across the top of the wooden crossing and glistening trails of freshly trodden grass beyond. The vague footmarks head across the field and further into the dark unknown.

He hiccups again and giggles to himself.

Brekk : **Ah fuck it.**

He climbs over the wet, muddy stile and lands in the overgrown grass beyond.

He marches purposefully into the moon-sprung darkness with another little giggle and a hiccup. The shadows and silhouettes of the hedgerows and woodlands consume him as he stumbles onward. The heavy skies edge back toward the moon as the darkness swirls about him.

A sudden surge of dark clouds and the moon hides itself completely, and blackest darkness returns to cloak the land and sky.

Brekk : (unseen in the darkness but crashing through the undergrowth) (hiccup) (burp) (giggle) **Here witchy, here little witchy....**

And on he goes, giggling and stumbling, merrily into the darkness.

Elsewhere

Amid the broad sparse landscape in the bowl of the valley, a large, roaring fire is encircled by a crowd that rumbles and bristles with anticipation. The hooded congregation mill and pulse. A naked procession swirls around the fire, an eclectic mix of fevered expression.

Next to this, around a tall wooden staging another crowd's increasingly vehement chanting demands congress.

The gathered crowds swarm as do the clouds about the peaking moon. The low chanting, pierced by impatient feral shrieks and animalistic calls, echoes through the black and silvering night sky. Heavy rain breaks above them and a drum beat strikes, inspiring wild, fresh fervour.

...

Brekk, still crashing through the undergrowth, has lost his merriment along with his inebriation. Shortly, everything but despair has deserted him.

Brekk : (fear) **Oh my god, oh my god. Fuck. Fuck. Fuck. I can't fucking see...oh fuck.**

Blindly crashing through some rough woodland, brambles arrest and pull; branches trip and soft ground brings him to a stumbling lurch. Frantically, painfully, he goes on. A thorny silhouette against a vaguely lesser darkness suggests a route from the thicket and he starts towards this desperate salvation.

He pulls himself from the grabbing undergrowth and lurches, stumbling into the open grassy plain where, realizing the weight of the rain…

Brekk : (a plea to the heavens) **Oh come on....**

Relieved to be out of the thicket he resigns himself to the weather and spins in the darkness. A howl echoes from…somewhere… and he turns, alarmed, peering into the messy black woodland behind him. He turns back and squints into the stubborn night, noticing a flickering tinge of light to the crest of the hill. A short trudge through the heavy grass should give him a view of the valley ahead.

Another noise, a scream or shriek perhaps. Brekk lifts his head, searching for the noise. Something rhythmic, barely audible, is pulsing through the air and Brekk narrows his eyes in puzzled concern. He looks again to the highlighted hilltop and his resolve returns. A deep breath and he strides toward the crested hill.

He moves slowly through the heavy, wet grass toward the dark summit.

As he nears, the vague noises and rhythms become louder, clearer, and Brekk's heart begins to race as he starts to imagine the sort of event from which these feral sounds could emanate. His pace quickens.

More impatient shrieks fill the air, chanting and a low drum beat. Brekk moves faster toward the brow of the hill and his eyes are full of intrigue as the noises resound more clearly about him. He sees the busy glow from some light source, hazing the night sky past the summit of the hill.

As he breaches the summit his expression reflects wonder at the site before him. There, low in the valley, the source of the sounds and luminance. A large flaming pyre, surrounded by naked writhing dancers. Around them a braying crowd awaits some ceremony as, to the side, a large wooden framework is attended to.

Another barrage of impatient screams fill the air and on the hilltop, alarmed, Brekk, ducks down into the long grass at his feet. His view now obscured he crawls forward, pushing the long, wet grass aside and wriggling into a patch of shorter grass and ferns.

Brekk's eyes are alive with excitement as, through the foliage, he watches the event unfold.

The swathes of hooded and cowled onlookers are equally entranced by the events and an explosion of light bursting from the centre of the dancing circle causes a reciprocal eruption of noise and excitement.

From nowhere, two cowled figures have appeared next to the large scaffold. Their sudden appearance shocks and quietens the crowd.

Glinting above them, the scaffold supports a series of large blades, all delicately strung and shining in the moonlight. Beneath the blades, lying prostrate, a hooded figure, unmoving, atop a wooden plinth. The two cowled figures move toward the still body. Taking small knives from inside their gowns they start to draw out symbols in the air.

The ring of naked dancers, their bodies painted by the flickering fire and moonlight, gyrate and writhe as the rhythms and pulsing beats quicken. Two of the dancers, overcome by the moment, fuck roughly on the ground as the others continue their fevered dance.

Approaching the recumbent, the two cowled figures stop. One toward the head the other at the feet. They spread their arms wide, the daggers reaching between them.

The crowd has quietened in expectation now, while above, Brekk bristles nervously.

Another flashy explosion and another person appears amid the staging to a cold sudden silence. He steps into the space between the two outstretched daggers. Reaching out his own arms so they form a triple crucifix, he takes the two daggers and steps forward to the side of the dais and the prone figure.

Above on the hillside, Brekk, wide-eyed and transfixed, breathless through fear of his understanding of what is about to happen suddenly remembers his phone and scrambles in the dark to fish it from his pocket.

Brekk : **Fuck, fuck, fuck. Fuck, this is it. Fucking hell... I've found it...** (he presses the power button on his phone) **Ariff, you fucker you won't believe this.**

Brekk looks up to see the masked figure bring his arms forward and plant the two daggers together. Grasping the combined hilt with both hands he lines up the tip over the still figure's heart.

Brekk : **Oh No !!!**

As Brekk's phone springs to life the screen lights up—twelve missed calls, all from Ariff. As the hooded figure lifts the blade in preparation Brekk hits the call button. He looks up.

The blades fall, pushed into the chest of the figure without a sound. A small convulsion of the limbs settles almost immediately.

All is silent in ceremonial reverence when, from the pocket of the sacrifice, a phone rings out. A chirping exaltation which slowly comes to a computer glitch of a finale. A comedy ringtone, Ariff's ring tone. Brekk furrows his already concerned brow in confusion. His breath and senses deserting him, he stares harder through the obscuring undergrowth. Below the hood he recognizes the t-shirt, Ariff's jeans, Ariff's lifeless body.

In the moonlight, Brekk is dumbstruck. All emotion drops from his face, his mind, all feeling leaves his body. Then he unwittingly stands up, a lone figure on the hillside amid waist-high ferns, unnoticed by the crowds below.

The three masked figures take a step backward away from the body; their arms still held aloft, they relax, then thrust their hands forward into the air as a loud exultation leaves their lips.

The large blades above the figure on the table fall. The head and limbs leave the table, rolling, then dropping into deftly crafted openings around the base of the plinth.

Brekk stumbles, his mind overwhelmed. From the depths of his being is welling some oral manifestation of pain and disbelief. As he opens his mouth a low rumble skreeks from his throat, building, building until... There is a flurry of movement behind him and all becomes thuddingly, painfully, black...

Ariff Saturday 30th

Brekk's eyes flash open. He is in bed, in the room at the B+B. He sits up and looks across the room to Ariff's bed, to the duvet stretched over Ariff's sleeping form.

Brekk : (collapsing back into his sweaty pit) **Fucking hell!**

He closes his eyes and, mumbling, goes back to sleep.

An hour or so passes.

The sun shines through the window and lights the room, a bright breezy morning to what can only be a bright, breezy, joyful day. Brekk's duvet is thrown forward as he sits up, spins and drops his legs over the edge of the bed.

Brekk : **Fuck me, I can't remember getting in...**

He stands up and breathes in the light and fresh air that's pouring through the window. He half yawns, shakes his head and shuffles into the small washroom.

He's brushing his teeth.

Brekk : **Those fucking witches got me pissed. I've no idea what it was but fuck, it gave me some vivid dreams.**

Brekk : **You'll never guess what I was dreaming about** (forget that) **That girl, from the pub, from here, she's interesting, and those old ladies, that's what I've been talking about.**

It's all muffled through toothpaste and brushing. He rinses and is clearer.

Brekk : **There's a link, you know, back to the 'earlier thinking'. They reckon the magic is gone but there's definitely something they're not telling me**. (he gazes at his reflection) **I think it's real, Ariff...** (then to himself) **It's real.**

He looks across from the washroom to Ariff's uninterested sleeping form.

Brekk : **Okay, what about you? I'll bet you got up to all sorts of nonsense.**

He continues his recollections to the sleeping Ariff. He stretches out his stiff neck, grimacing as he does.

Brekk : **Christ I've got a bad head. I even dreamt I'd been cracked over the bonce.** (then rhetorical) **Why would you dream that?**

He winces as vague memories contort his features. Looking in the mirror now, he lifts his hand to the back of his head and runs his fingers through some matted hair...

Brekk : **Youch!**

He looks at his fingers, dried flakes and a sweaty smear of blood.... He looks out at the view of Ariff's sleeping body, his gaze quickly moving up the resting form. He stares intently at the duvet and his skin shudders as he realises there is no movement from beneath. His eyes narrow and a grimace twists his features as he clumsily drops his toothbrush into the basin and he slowly moves toward the bed.

Brekk : **Ariff?**

His unenthusiastic hand reaches out to the crumpled bed cover and his fingers take a gentle hold at the edge. He stares at it.

He takes a breath. He's not ready, another breath. He yanks on the corner of the duvet and it reveals its contents. The duvet was merely resting, as it had fallen when Ariff threw it down the night before, resting over Ariff's case and strewn clothes.

Downstairs, at the reception desk in the B+B, Brekk rounds the corner at the bottom of the stairs and starts slapping the bell on the counter.

Brekk : **Hello ....hello .... fucking come on ...Hello!** (he peers about in desperation)

Brekk runs out into the street. He looks around and, running to the first corner, he turns to see this road is as empty as the last. He remembers his phone and grabs for his pocket. He lifts the phone to see it is out of battery.

Brekk : **Fuck! For fuck's sake.**

He runs from one street to the next. A phone box! Another distressed dash.

Of course, the public phone doesn't work.

Brekk : **Fuck!!!**

He considers smashing the handset but, grimacing, slowly returns it to its receiver. His head drops forward onto the phone as desperation clouds his thoughts and he slowly turns his head as a long sigh slips from his lips.

In the distance—his eyes narrow—is that Cerrick?

He leaps from the phone box and calls out as he lurches down the road. The figure in the distance seems to turn and look toward his loud exclamation but then turns away and, at Brekk's lumpen arrival, there is no one to be found.

His frustrations overloaded and heart achingly distraught he turns to find he is outside of the Police station. **The Police. The Police!** He lets out a heavy breath of relief and tries to peer through one of the small windows. He can't see any signs of life but he hammers the heavy brass knocker and waits. No answer. He seems more prepared for the disappointment and knocks again. As he wanders off, a small curtain near the door draws to one side.

The sun continues to shine.

A moment of stillness and Brekk finds himself sitting on an old bench, he pulls his phone from his pocket then remembers tucking the charger into the glove box in Ariff's van.

Brekk : (of course) **The van!**

He heads back to the B+B and then around the back where Ariff had parked. He stops in his tracks as he sees the van is gone. He looks down to the puddly ground and notices the van has splashed out one of the deep puddles that pock mark the rough yard. The wet tyre marks are intermittent but show which direction the van took and he starts to follow them. They quickly dry and diminish to nothing, leaving him disheartened at the outskirts of the small hamlet.

Brekk : **What the fuck is going on?**

Now ambling, he heads back into the street and starts walking. He stops, closes his eyes and takes another deep breath as he tries to clear his head. As he opens his eyes, he sees one of the old women from the pub. He tries to shout but his voice catches and fails to project. Desperate for her attention he runs and catches up to her just as she is disappearing through a gnarled old doorway.

Brekk : (out of breath) **Help me, please…**

Misty : (looks slightly disappointed that he has managed to catch her) **What is it lovey?**

Brekk : **My friend he's, well I think he's been… last night up on the hill, there were all these witches and a ceremony, my friend, I think he was...**

Misty : **You were on your own last night, sweetheart.**

Brekk : **He'd gone…before…please.**

Misty : **Well don't worry lovey, I'm sure he's fine, why don't you try and find him?**

Brekk : **But I am.**

She is closing the door as she backs into the building,

Misty : **I'm sure everything is as it should be** (then, less convincing) **It will probably be fine.**

And the door is shut. He can't believe the lack of concern or help and stutters in exasperation but finds no words. He resigns himself to walking away but he pulls himself back and knocks. He waits. He tries again. Nothing.

Fuck!

Propped in the window a recipe book, though covered in dust, triggers some train of thought.

Then, Inspiration! **The Pub!**

He gets his bearings and slowly starts to work out the route they had taken to the pub.

More country lanes.

Brekk stands at the door to the Wizards Tipp. Like all of the other local shops and businesses he has seen, the pub is closed. He peers through the window, resigned to the fact that it will be deserted. He circles to the back of the building. Re-finding the overgrown path he follows it through the lane at the rear of the terrace, then crosses the rough access area. He spots the deep puddle he had sunk into and deftly hops over it before climbing the wooden stile into the fields. He follows the path of trodden grass his senses prickling in anticipation. In the daylight he easily recognises the tangle of woodland which had treated him so badly and he circumnavigates it to re-join his path up the hill.

As he approaches the hilltop his pulse begins to quicken and he slows as he breaches the crest. He looks down to the fields below and the now bare site. His stomach knots and he grimaces involuntarily as images of the braying crowds and glinting blades overwhelm him. Dropping to one knee he takes a couple of deep breaths to calm himself. He shakes his head in disbelief but stands, resolve intact. In the daylight he sees how the valley sides and a few solitary hills conclude the majesty of this natural amphitheatre. He traverses the valley, wading through long grass and lumpen earth, down toward the valley floor.

From his elevated view he sees a charred fire pit and heavily trampled grass are the only evidence of his nightmare. A veil of dread has descended as he steps into the fields of the valley floor. His footsteps pull him over the site and he finds himself drawn to where he feels the most horrific part of the event took place. He drops to his knees and feels the grass before him. A deep melancholy has dawned, along with an acid disbelief. He drags himself back to his feet. As he stands, he feels the ground beneath him shift a little. Provoked, he stamps to test the surface. A hollow clang emanates from the earth and he realises he is above a covered opening. He falls back to his knees and grabs at the turf. It rolls back to uncover some large rough hinges and, exploring further, tightly woven ribbons of metal cage doors, a large padlock holds them shut.

He looks around for inspiration when a screech alerts him to the outskirts of the open ground. A vehicle, laden with weirdos, and carrying several scaffolding poles has skidded to a halt and the passengers are jumping from the bed of the truck. Other similarly laden vehicles are following them into the field.

Brekk, already on his knees, hits the floor flat on his front, pulls back the roll of turf to cover the lock and doors then scrambles toward some scrubland across the muddy field. From the cover of the scrubland, he wriggles toward the hedge.

Happy that he is hidden, he turns to watch as the group, having disembarked, start to look across the field. One of the men is pointing toward Brekk and the others all start toward him. Brekk turns away and in desperation he forces himself through a sparse section of the hedge. The hedge snags at his clothes and panic floods his system until he realises the men have stopped at the loose turf area. They appear to be measuring and marking out some future development; others are dragging scaffolding poles from the truck. He wriggles from the last grabbing twigs and thorns and rolls off the grass verge to find himself on a tarmacked lane. He skulks away along the narrow road before taking a last look at the site while brushing himself down. He turns now, determined.

The Police Station

Brekk approaches the heavy, police station door with fresh purpose. He reaches for the large brass knob but before he can grab it the door springs open and out of the darkness a tall, impressive looking police officer steps into the light. The officer squints in the sunlight and, placing his cap firmly on his head, he turns back toward the door as a smaller officer appears. The taller, superior officer nods toward him.

Tall Officer : **I take it I've made myself clear?**

Shorter Officer : (stiffening) **Yes Sir, of course...** (he spots Brekk waiting in anticipation and grimaces at the silent interruption)

The taller officer, noticing this disrespect, throws a stern look at the subordinate who quickly adjusts his attitude.

Tall Officer : (turning to leave) **I'll leave you gentlemen to your business.** (He nods a flinty goodbye towards Brekk and strides away into the distance before rounding the corner of the building)

Brekk's expression turns forlorn at this departure. He looks back at the somewhat desperate figure left before him.

The further away the superior officer gets the less sincere the remaining officer's demeanour becomes, until eventually any compulsion toward civility has dissolved.

Officer : (frothing with disdain) **What do you want ?**

Brekk : (Visibly shaken) **My, um, friend, I think, I think he's been killed...**

Officer : (suddenly serious) **Oh!** (he turns and heads inside) **Come on.**

The officer closes the flap of the dark wooden counter he has stepped behind and pulls a book from somewhere underneath.

Officer : (flustered) **Um, do we need an ambulance or something? I mean, are you sure he's dead?**

Brekk : (His expression turns grave) **They cut his head off!**

Officer : **His head?**

Brekk : **And his arms and legs...**

Officer : (a hint of incredulity) **Really?**

Brekk nods silently while he recalls the scene.

Officer : **Right, I won't bother with the ambulance...** (he purses his lips in a spasm of scepticism) **Lets take some details, shall we.**

He lifts his pen as he opens the notebook.

Officer : **Where did this occur?**

Brekk : (slightly desperate) **I don't really know the area...um...**

The officer gestures to a large, black and white topographical map that fills the wall at the end of the counter.

Brekk steps up to the map and starts to get his bearings. He finds the village then traces his path from the pub. He sees the village hall where Ariff had stayed at the party. He finds the route he now knows he took, and the path to the top of the small hill where he overlooked the ceremony.

Brekk : (points out his position at the crest of the hill) **Here, I was here, but he was down there.**

Officer : **The Manor House.**

Brekk : **No, there's no house there.**

Officer : **No, not any more...**

He turns and reaches up to prise a book from one of the many shelves behind the reception desk. He puts it down on the counter and flicks through the tome where he finds some sketchy schematics of a large manor house. Several other papers fall from within the cover and spread over the desk.

Officer : **Here, look.** (he points to the illustration until Brekk, nodding, homes in on the right page)

Officer : **And when did this death occur?**

Brekk : **Last night.**

Officer : **Last Night?** (there is a strange tone to his response which catches Brekk's attention)

Brekk : **Yes, midnight.**

Officer : **Last night? Midnight?**

Brekk : **Yes.**

Officer : **Hmmn.** (he puts down the pen) **And what happened exactly**?

Brekk : **Yes... Um. We'd been out and met up with some, well um, witches** (*Witches*!) **Ugh, yes and Ariff** (*That's your friend's name*?) **Yes, yes. Ariff, stayed with a group of younger, um, witches but I followed one up to the top of that** (he points back to the map) **hill and I saw them, they were doing spells and there was chanting and a crowd. Then a wizard or, or something appeared out of nowhere and, and they had him laid out and... and they cut him into pieces!**

Officer : (eyes Brekk with intense scrutiny then..) **Wait here.**

He turns and heads out through a door behind him.

Brekk watches him leave, then turns his attention back to the book and the diagrams of the manor house. One of the loose drawings shows a large stately manor nestled in the valley at the exact spot where the ceremony had taken place. And Brekk sees, beneath the house, the dotted lines marking a tunnel leading away from the house before turning slightly to head toward the outline of a large, circular cellar. He looks in bemuzement at the unusual subterranean construction and notices it is two stories connected by two small stairwells on the outside and at opposite sides of the rooms.

He starts to consider the relevance of this structure, places his finger to mark the drawing and looks up, anticipating the officer's return.

The officer is standing inches from Brekk, a strange look on his face.

Officer : **Is this him?**

Brekk : **Eh?**

Officer : (placing a jar down on the desk) **Is. This. Him?**

Brekk, flummoxed, looks at the officer, then down to the jar that has been plonked squarely on the book.

Brekk : **Eh?**

In the jar a large grey-green toad wriggles as it climbs onto a bit of stick that protrudes from the dull water that half fills the container.

Brekk looks up at the officer, still dumbstruck.

Officer : **No? What about this, is this him?**

And he produces another jar. This one contains a newt.

Brekk, still unsure of what is going on, purses his lips as he tries to form a question that resists its own creation.

Officer : **No? Well perhaps it's the girl from last year or the kid from the summer?**

Brekk : **Wha..**?

Officer : (who can hardly contain his rising ire) **Just fuck off. Go, on. Get the fuck out of here.** (he's lifting the flap in the worktop)

Brekk, realising the amount of aggression bubbling within the officer starts toward the door. A flurry of arms and the book and jar fall from the counter…

Officer : (making a wild grab for the darting Brekk) **Fucking students.**

Brekk is through the door and quickly a short distance from the station. Breathing heavily, he turns to see the officer framed in the doorway, still ranting.

Officer : **Every fucking year. Can't throw them in the fucking brook. Fucking evidence? Fucking evidence that you lot are a bunch of wanking, shithouses.** (he seems to suddenly remember something, furtively looks left and right then ducks back into the police station as his tirade degenerates into mumbling..) **I'd turn you into a fucking toad. Think we're stupid country folk…I'm not even from round here. I'm from fucking London!**

Brekk, shuffling away, looks down to see he is still holding one of the pages and he stuffs it into his pocket. He looks back and watches as the door is slammed shut. From behind the door, one last verbal expulsion reverberates through the building.

: **SHITHOUSES!**

...

The weather has started to turn and a sharp cold wind is whipping about a shell-shocked Brekk. Despondent, he decides to make his way back to the B+B, his brow furrowed. He is now freshly weary about the village and all its inhabitants.

Strolling back he rounds another corner to see, in the distance, another little old lady. She ambles around a corner into an alley, her shawl drawn up tightly over her head. He considers the wasted effort but then reluctantly jogs toward the junction, he half calls as he nears the opening.

From down the alley there is a loud vociferous expulsion and before Brekk can turn into the alleyway...

A voice : **Fuck! I haven't got time for this**...

Cerrick emerges from the alley, almost crashing into Brekk.

Cerrick : **You!**

Brekk halts, as surprised as she is. He glances over her shoulder but there is no sign of the old lady.

Cerrick : **Get out, and stay out of my way!**

Brekk : **Please. My friend. Please.**

His pleading catches her off guard and she considers him for a moment.

Cerrick : **Are you serious?**

Brekk : **What d'you mean?**

Cerrick : **You! Are you serious?**

They eye each other with searing intensity.

Brekk : (fiercely earnest) **Yes. Yes, I am.**

Cerrick : (this is food for thought) **Just stay out of the way.**

She starts to barge past him.

Brekk : **But...**

Cerrick : (as she strides off) **There's no time. Just stay out of the way.**

He watches in deep frustration as she goes.

Unsettled, completely confused and utterly forlorn, he slowly heads back to the B+B.

At the counter there is no sign of the old lady, for which he is grateful, and he quietly climbs the stairs to his room. He stands at the doorway, surveying the room's contents. A morbid resignation has overcome him and he steps into the room and starts throwing his and Ariff's gear into their bags.

He throws the holdalls over his shoulder and slowly makes his way down the stairs. As he's passing the reception desk, a creak from the shadows, the old woman appears behind him. He does not see her, though he does sense something and stops in his tracks, dropping the bags as he does so.

Behind him, her hand reaches out slowly and her cold fingers wrap around his wrist, scaring the air from his lungs and what remains of the sanity from his mind. He stands rigid with fright.

Lilly : **I've got something for you, lovely.**

She holds up a piece of paper with a number scrawled across it. She reads the words on the note.

Lilly : **Call this number.**

She pushes the note into his frozen hand.

He stands with the note held aloft, still rigid.

The old lady releases her grip and disappears back into the shadows, a door creaks open then closes behind her.

Brekk, alone and with air refilling his lungs, looks at the paper.

Brekk : **But....**

He looks around.

The old lady pokes her head around the creaky door,

Lilly : **You can use our phone lovely...**

And she points to the old Bakelite phone on the counter. She closes the door and is gone.

What and Why Saturday 30th 8pm

Brekk : (the phone to his ear) **YOU!**

Ariff has answered the phone.

Ariff : **Hey, hiya, Brekk, you coming to the pub?**

Brekk : (angry and relieved) **Where the fuck have you been? I've been...I've....** (He doesn't finish the thought)

Ariff : (whispering) **Mate, I've found some...** (*Some what*?) **I've...er, met some people I think you'll find quite interesting....**

...

A long walk to the pub. Brekk has pushed through a torrent of rain and wind. The village and roads are cast into near darkness; it is early evening and the sky is thick with rainclouds.

The door to the pub swings open before him. From inside he is silhouetted in the doorway as a bolt of lightning erupts in the faraway hills. The door rattles and the sound of the battering rain fills the public house. The room is full of the coven guys and girls from the rave, and as then, they now surround Ariff. They stand in a quickly settling silence, curious as to who has come to meet their new 'friend'. The rain falls from Brekk's long coat in a persistent torrent.

Ariff : (breaking this bristling anticipation) **Is it still raining?**

The room erupts with laughter and Brekk raises his eyes to the ceiling,

Brekk : **Oh, great.**

He steps into the busy room.

Ariff jumps up to greet him and pulls him through the throng, pausing for a few brief introductions. As he goes, Brekk recognises more of the faces from the rave the evening before.

The group welcome Brekk enthusiastically, ignoring his obvious, though tacit discomfort.

While Ariff commands the attention of the small group that surrounds him, Brekk notices another man has entered the room. Older, good-looking, charm oozes from every pore. There are two deputies at this man's shoulder and, as he mixes through the congregation, the interest of the room quickly shifts from Brekk and Ariff to this newcomer. Brekk also notices a reciprocal interest and, as Brekk watches him, this 'celebrity' turns to eye Brekk's own advance through the room. They nod a small acknowledgment before the older man turns back to the fawning crowd. All crave his attention.

Ariff, extracting himself from the fuss, pulls Brekk over to one side, pushing a pathway through and toward a quieter section of the pub lounge. Still, the girls are flashing beautiful, flirty smiles towards Ariff and he, as ever, enjoys the attention. As they head toward their quiet retreat Brekk sees, in the far corner of the room, a mannequin. Dressed in the clothes Ariff had worn the night before.

Brekk : (remembering his concern) **Ariff. I saw... I thought I saw you killed last night!**

Ariff : (unconcerned) **No, no. It was him.** (he points to the mannequin) **I'm all right. Look!**

He lifts his arms as if to show Brekk his completeness. Brekk takes a longer look at the mannequin and sees it is crudely stitched back together.

Ariff : **This is it Brekk, this why we came! This is why you wanted to come.**

Brekk : (eyeing the mannequin) **Hey, my shirt!**

Ariff : **This is who you have been looking for. All your questions can be answered here!**

Brekk : (starting to listen to Ariff) **Really**!! **So, what was that about? Why did they kill you, well, him?** (he nods toward the dummy)

Ariff : **Acceptance. Trust. Preparation. That sort of stuff...**

Brekk : **But... What...?**

Ariff : **There is to be a full ceremony.** (he tries to remember the information) **It's a major step in the coven's reformation. We're all going to be a part of it. You too... If you want.**

Brekk : **What?**

Ariff : (he attempts seriousness) **The ceremonies purpose is, er,** (he struggles to remember) **to present the coven's chosen one, an immortal leader who would lead the coven into the 21st century, to kickstart the reformation of the pagan religion, to reengage the people with the magic that was once a powerful force for good in the world. The members of this coven will be first wave of generals at his, The Chosen One's, side.** (he looks smug at his recital)

Brekk looks at the older man and his deputies disparagingly,

Brekk : **Oh I see, and he's The Chosen One is he? Smarmy git, just cos he's kept his...**(begrudgingly).... **looks. God it's depressing. Even followers of...natural religion, fall for a cheesy smile and slight...I don't know, charming demeanour. Is that all you need to be 'The Chosen One', charm?**

Ariff : **No, no, it's not him... he has been the organizer, the instigator, a, er, conduit for the knowledge, preparing the coven for the right time.**

Brekk : **Oh, and what makes this the right time?**

Ariff : **Well, It's not so much the time that's important...more a case of the right circumstance and a, uh, conjunction of the right elements....**

Brekk : **Conjunction, eh...hmmm, and what are the right elements? Enough busty vacuous girls hanging around...** (he looks about the room) **enough knuckleheads around for the 'chosen one' to feel protected?**

Ariff : **They're good people Brekk, they're intelligent...kind...educated...um, interesting, loyal.**

Brekk : **Sheesh...been busy with you haven't they?**

Ariff : **Look, these people, this coven, have been organizing... preparing. They've been waiting, waiting for the RIGHT** (he fixes Brekk with a stare) **person...someone with the Right understanding!**

Brekk : (his interest is suddenly engaged) **The *right* person!**

Ariff, nods a little, and continues,

Ariff : **A person with the right interest, the right demeanour, the ability to become their new leader.**

Brekk : **A person with the right understanding, eh...really?. The ability, um...gravitas, to become their new leader, did you say immortal? Immortal in a mythic sense, someone who'll make their mark, who will have the strength to make decisions that will stand the tests of time, yes: a very...very special person.**

Ariff : **The ceremony! This person, will be reborn, reborn as 'The One', a vessel for the power of the craft.**

Brekk : **Reborn, how reborn?!!!**

Ariff : **Well, okay, first things first. Giving up all worldly possessions, but...**

Brekk : (to himself) **Well, if they didn't have much anyway.**

Ariff : **Yeah, all worldly possessions...um, *everything physical I think he said...***

Brekk : **Yes, I understand. A clean slate...so as to be able to concentrate on the relevant...the pertinent. A leader cannot be... distracted by their own, personal mundanities.**

Ariff : **Um, yeah I guess...I knew you'd understand.**

Brekk : **Well, of course...not everyone, has the...right qualities.**

Ariff : **And of course the reborn leader would need trusted friends..., a circle of the most intelligent, loyal followers close to him...**

Brekk : **Well I'm sure people who were loyal,** (looking at Ariff quizzically) **you know I don't know how important, um, intelligence, not, you know, that sort of obvious intelligence would necessarily be the precise quality to worry about!**

He puts his hand on Ariff's shoulder and gives him a sympathetic but warmish smile.

Brekk : **But loyalty, and a social prowess, yes, that would be very important, valuable...**

Ariff is now looking at Brekk quizzically. Something about this conversation is troubling him, and he is about to say something when,

Devvin : **Hello Brekk.**

The older fellow with the two deputies has stepped up to the pair as they have been talking and, with a huge friendly smile, is offering Brekk his hand.

Brekk's hand fills the open palm automatically. He is spun around, the man's arm falls around his shoulder, and they are suddenly walking together like the oldest of friends. Behind them Ariff is engulfed in a mass of friendly, female flesh.

Devvin : **Ariff told me all about you. I expect he has explained the situation?**

Brekk : **Yes, yes, we've just been...he's a good old friend of mine, um...** (he looks across at Ariff, trying to convey a sense of affection) **We've known each other a long time.**

Devvin : **Yes, good, good. it's unusual you know, we would have waited but, to find someone with all the right qualities, how exciting. We** (he gestures towards his two deputies) **have been training up the most forward of this coven, preparing them until it would become obvious which should be chosen. There are always hurdles and, of course, the one big one, the next one!** (he nods at Brekk, encouraging his affirmation) **But then, incredibly, the right person walks through the door, just fantastic. And just at the right time.**

Brekk : **The right time?**

Devvin : **Oh yes , we can take advantage of the forthcoming cross quarter**.

Brekk : **Samhain! Yes, of course...right...hang on, that's tomorrow isn't it?**

Devvin : **Oh yes...we were working, hoping to have developed someone for this time a year from now, but I'm sure you'll agree that the sooner this takes place the sooner we can start the resurgence, and I don't think that it's a coincidence, do you? The Mother provides.**

Devvin looks up, evoking the sense of some higher power at work.

Brekk : (copying Devvin's upward gaze) **Um, no, I'm sure. Um, just quickly, how does the rebirthing ceremony work?**

Devvin : **Yes, I understand your concern, and, when you are fully aware of the nature of the old magic you will see why it's so unusual to find someone who is ready, personally ready, without the training and education involved. The rebirthing ceremony will be a shedding of the old, a freeing of the spirit and a rebirth, fresh and new and unhindered. You understand?**

Brekk : **Yes, yes. Um. But, how is the 'shedding' done? Is it perhaps hypnotism...or...or a textual reading, a submersion into the teachings of obliterating the conscious mind?**

Devvin : **Oh no....All physical presence must be extinguished, to leave only the spirit, the spirit which can then be cleansed. Only then can we move forward.**

Brekk : **Extinguished??? Death!!!!!**

Devvin : **Only physically.**

Brekk : **You're talking about actual Death!! You have to actually die to become immortal...what sort of immortality is that? Are you crazy?**

Devvin : **Ah yes, the common reaction...but what you are missing, what *you* do not yet understand...is the fact that once your spirit has been cleansed, it is summoned back to the physical, renewed, untainted and perfect as in the beginning. This is the power of this craft, the power of this lore. Samhain is, as you know, when the veil between our world and the next is at its most vulnerable. Allowing for the soul to depart and return in its most pure iteration**.

Brekk : (looks horrified) **No way! No way.**

Devvin : **Your reaction illustrates why it is so unusual to find one so perfect, so primed, so full of the necessary belief.** (He turns to look at Ariff) **He truly is The Chosen One.**

Ariff, from amongst the adoring mass, waves enthusiastically, a big, generous, contented smile across his face.

A Dispute

Brekk : **They're going to KILL you ....AGAIN, properly, this time. Fucking Dead!**

Ariff : **But it's not even *dead* dead is it!** (he smiles) **It's not permanent. And then when I'm…returned…you know…my spirit...back to the physical...then I will be...um…immortal.**

Brekk : (mocking Ariffs tone) **'um...immortal'. And you believe all this? It's…** (he looks around at the vapid gathering) **fucking nonsense!**

Ariff : **No, it's not. And you believed it a minute ago when you thought it was you! Look, its exactly like you said, belief is part of the er necessary…conditions for it to work.... It is all true, Brekk. And...when I am returned, not only am I immortal, but… Look, It's not about facts and knowledge. It's about 'belief'. At the moment only the elder is actually complete, but after the ceremony all those who take part will start their journey, their...education.**

Brekk : **Hang on, you didn't have a clue about this stuff a couple of days ago…and, and now you're the…fucking 'Chosen One'. And, and talking about your coven's development and *you're going to let them kill you...*fuck, Ariff! You don't actually *know* if any of this is real.**

Ariff : **It is real, I know it.**

Brekk : **What d'you mean you *know it*? What have you seen that lets you know it?**

Ariff : **Devvin, the older guy, he's shown me libraries of books.**

Brekk : **What about magic? Has he shown you true magic?**

Ariff : **Ah now, he could only show me small, 'actual magic'.**

Brekk **: Small magic?**

Ariff : **Yeah, small magic.**

Brekk : **Oh god.** (exasperated) **Tricks. He's shown you a few tricks.**

Ariff : (earnestly) **No, no. This was real magic. I swear. But only small stuff.**

Brekk : (incredulous) **Right, right. Yeah, just the small stuff. And why not 'The Big Stuff'?**

Ariff : **Because he has to allow my belief to prove itself. If I need proof then I wouldn't need my belief. You know, like you said!**

Brekk : **So what has he shown you?**

Ariff : **Hmmn,** (he considers the things he has seen) **Hard to explain but there are libraries and archives and examples of, you know. It's just real.**

Brekk : (shaking his head) **Are you sure you're up to the task they're asking of you, because to be honest, you know...this seems to be a bit beyond what you're used to...**

Ariff **: This is beyond what anyone's used to...**

Brekk : **Yeah, very good. But, he said *you* were ready, primed. What makes you so special? He was telling me they've been preparing their own, for a year from now and then you turn up and you're straight to the front of the class... You!! ... I know people generally like you, but fuckin' hell. 'He's quite nice, let's make him immortal'.!!** (he's gotten angry and frustrated) **It's like, fuck... *You've* cast a spell on them! Like you do on all the stupid, pretty girls and fatherless idiots out there. A friendly, non-judgmental, successful...socially successful...simplefuckington!... Jees, is that all it takes, is that all they yearn after or aspire to? Yes, yes...of course...you're nothing but a mirror for their vacuity...they see you as a celebrity...with your pretty face and...and unchallenging...*easy*.........**

Ariff : (happily nodding along, but then) **Yeah, just hang on a minute...I don't think that's it actually,...it's a funny thing. You know when I had to put your shirt, your T-shirt on—the one you've drawn all over—well that was what started them off, the drawings.**

Brekk : **What drawings?** (realization) **The symbols, the old symbols for regeneration and enlightenment and, and...Wow...of course they recognized them!**

Ariff : **Yeah...well then they were talking about magic and stuff and I was explaining, you know, about how belief is a subconscious part of the elements, the, er, fundamentals, to the um...what makes it all work…**

Brekk : **To the success of the incantation or ceremony or spell or whatever…**

Ariff : **Yeah, yeah .. like what you were talking about...and then they were saying that the biggest hurdle to finding someone willing to do it is the death part, but I'm like 'no, no, death is nothing to be afraid of', and like I said, we've all been dead before,**

Brekk : **Hang on a minute...!There has been a mistake, a big one...Ariff, you know what's happened don't you? I mean, you can see it can't you...?**

Ariff looks puzzled: no he can't see it, and starts to slowly shake his head at Brekk.

Brekk : (to himself) **It is me!...It is meant to be me...** (then confidently) **I *should* be the chosen one...**

Ariff : **Hang on a minute, I don't think the chosen one's allowed to choose themselves.**

He looks around for some kind of confirmation.

From across the room the two deputies recognize some angst upon Ariff's features and start toward them.

Brekk : **You can see can't you? It's meant to be me. It's *my* shirt, *I'm* the one who understands this stuff, they're *my* theories you've impressed them with,**

Ariff : **Hey, that was my idea about being dead before!**

Brekk : (angry again) **Oh yes, well done...well done for contributing one fucking idea to a conversation... congratulations.... I know, to reward you let's make you ...*imfuckingmortal*......**

Ariff : **You don't even like these people.**

Brekk : (patronizing) **Of course I do**.... (He can't keep it up and has a change of mind). **Look, it's not about liking, it's...it's about being the right person for the job. I'm the one who understands.**

Ariff : **Look Brekk, I know you'd like to be mister popular for once but, this isn't about that, it's...**

The deputies arrive at Ariff's shoulder.

Deputy 1 : (the hiss is heavy) **Is everything alright, sir? Wou ....**

Brekk : **Sir!... fucking 'sir'!!...you're fucking joking...**

Ariff : **Hey, come on...calm down...**

Brekk : **Calm fucking down...you're a fucking joke, an...**

One of the deputies reaches up to Brekk's straining neck and gently squeezes some hidden pressure point. He is suddenly frozen, his whole head, neck and shoulders stuck in a furious grimace as he was about to sputter some torrent of ill-considered abuse.

He is spun around and frog-marched through the meeting room and through the mass of now disapproving-looking men and women of the coven.

His grimace is still frozen into his features. As he passes through the group, he notices Cerrick talking to the other deputy, and he squeals through rigid lips. She sees him but looks away, unconcerned.

At the door the two hooded deputies nod to a couple of the guys and they step up and take hold of Brekk. The deputies head back to retake their positions at the sides of the elder, Devvin.

The pub door slams behind them and they are outside in the rain. Brekk is bundled into the back of a car, and driven around through the cobbled streets and dark country lanes until, thankfully, he recognizes the sign to the B+B.

The car screeches to a halt and the two goons pull themselves from their seats.

The back door is opened and Brekk, his face still locked mid-spasm, is unceremoniously thrown to the floor.

One of the guys turns to the other,

Goon1 : **Do you think you should release it? Do you even know how?**

Goon2 : **It'd be fun not to.**

Goon1 : **Do you know how not to?**

Goon2 : (perplexed at this double confusion) **How not to?**

Brekk looks up at them from the floor where he has landed in a puddle, the palsy still contorting his features. But a horrified sadness projects from his eyes as he realizes they're considering leaving him like this.

The young acolyte crouches down next to Brekk.

Goon2 : **Your friend's about to become a big thing around here. I'd consider working on your level of respect if I were you.**

He reaches across Brekk's shoulder and squeezes his neck. Brekk's locked features are suddenly free and he shouts...

Brekk : ***And you two wankers*** (the venom with which the words are projected declines rapidly, turning, by the end of the sentence, into almost a question) **can fuck off too....?**

The two look to each other and then back to Brekk, their faces stone cold.

Brekk : (sheepishly) **Sorry, that's what I was saying before...in the pub...to the other two.**

The deputies look at each other and burst out laughing. The car doors slam and the car screeches away throwing waves of muddy water over Brekk as he tries to get to his feet and find his balance. He slowly manages to stand, physically and mentally sodden.

Brekk : **Fuck.**

He turns slowly and trudges towards the door of the B+B.

Cerrick disturbs Brekk's evening

Brekk sits on his bed, soaked and despondent. The events of the last couple of days ricochet through his mind as he takes deep breaths while trying to find some sense of understanding. The door to his room creaks open; silhouetted against the bright landing is the old lady from downstairs. He is alarmed but seems resigned to the intrusion; she shuffles in toward him as his eyes betray his confusion until she passes him a large tankard of some hot, steamy, liquid which he is happy and quickly grateful to receive.

Shem : **You found your friend then, lovely?**

Brekk nods and shrugs at the same time. She looks about to tell him something when the bell on the counter downstairs rings and the old lady shuffles out.

He is drinking from the tankard and yawns joyously, the hot drink bringing more comfort than expected.

A short while later and he's stepping out of the steamy shower room, less weary and a little refreshed. He slides open the drawer from the small pine unit and shuffles through some pamphlets. He draws a couple from the pile and spaces them out on the grainy top. A bus timetable and a railway guide stare up at him. He sees the railway booklet is twenty years out of date and he drops it in the small bin. He scours the bus timetable while wondering if it is indeed still relevant, then taps it a couple of times before squaring it to the corner of the cabinet top for later consideration. He lets out a long sigh of disappointment and starts preparing for bed.

Brekk reaches down to pick up some pyjamas when he hears footsteps coming up the stairs towards his door. He softly steps to the door and pushes it firmly, but quietly, shut and gently slides the latch across.

There is a quiet tap at the door, Brekk, makes an actorly attempt at a snore then waits.

From outside : **It's me ..... Cerrick!**

Brekk : (suspiciously) **What? Why? What do you want?**

Cerrick : **Look, I know what's happening. I heard you...back at the pub. You're right, it should be you.**

Brekk opens the door, his eyes peering out with steely suspicion.

Brekk : **It should?**

Cerrick barges into the room...

Cerrick : **Yes, of course. Your friend, Ariff, is a simple man and not without his, obvious charms, and I know his heart is in the right place,... but the thought of someone so...** (she thinks for a moment) **Shallow! being a central figure in leading the reformation is ridiculous**. (Brekk is nodding along enthusiastically as she struts about the room). **You are better equipped to lead these people...to help recreate the craft...for more people. To help people understand how it can help society, the world.**

Cerrick : Devvin, talks about 'The Craft' helping the world, but to do that would take a serious person, a sensible person...someone untainted by Devvin's vision. (she spins toward Brekk)

Brekk is dumbstruck in the face of this outburst!

Cerrick : **We will swap you for your friend!**

Brekk : **Buh...Um...Uh...** (eventually) **How?**

Cerrick : **Hmmn, I'm working on it.**

Brekk : (he lets out a large sigh) **Wow! So, it really is all true. Magic and Witches and...**

Cerrick : **Of course**. (She turns to him then gravely) **You do believe, don't you? If you don't...**

Brekk : **Oh yes, of course , I was just checking on you...**

Cerrick : (stern) **Don't worry about me. But you, when you're faced with oblivion...You know true belief is necessary...**

Brekk : (he interrupts) **Yes, of course, it's fine.**

He turns away as his eyes betray a small glimmer of doubt.

Cerrick stares at him, sensing his uncertainty. She is about to confront him when he turns…

Brekk : **The women...the old women. Why aren't they more? Doing more? Involved more?**

Cerrick : **Hmmn.** (she considers her response) **What they told you is true. About the old magic dying. But…**

Brekk : **But why don't they believe in the same magic that, that…**

Cerrick : **Devvin!**

Brekk : **Yes, that prick. Why don't they believe in the same magic that he does?**

Cerrick : **They think…** (concerned pause) **they just think he's a charlatan.**

Brekk : **But you don't?**

Cerrick starts to strut back and fore once more and Brekk studies her intently.

Cerrick : **I know there's stuff they don't tell me. It's complicated, but I've lived here ever since I can remember, and I know there's more. They try to protect me from it, but I think that has blinded them to this, this threat. A threat that could** (she tries to find another word but fails) **threaten** (they share a glance which acknowledges the awkwardness) **their own existence. If he succeeds in creating this hierarchy and builds it into a movement...Well, who knows. That's why it has to be you, Brekk. Other than Ariff, you may be the only other person who has the necessary understanding combined with the belief to see this through...**

Brekk : (hmmn) **What about you?**

Cerrick : **Eh?**

Brekk : **What about you?**

Cerrick : (she considers this before..) **I'm afraid there are complications**... (she looks mournful as she considers them before turning enthusiastic) **But, we have a real opportunity here. You would be in an unprecedented position of influence...**

Brekk : **If it does work, won't there...**

Cerrick : (stern) **What do you mean, 'if'?**

Brekk : **Sorry, I mean, when. When it's done...** (he sees her concern) **It's just a turn of phrase, you know...**

Cerrick : (angry) **Well, 'turns of phrase' have power. Words have power.**

Brekk : **Yes. Of course. Sorry.**

Cerrick **:** (still angry and building) **You are going to have to be better than this. You will be in a position of great influence and every word you utter will be considered—and maybe acted upon—by a very broad range of people with a very broad range of intelligence and maybe disparate intent! Your vagueness and confusion are the seeds of future antagonisms.** (Brekk starts to respond but Cerrick isn't finished) **Using unclear language is the tool of the fool, the charlatan, and the narcissist. And there are already too many of those…** (she searches for the right term) **Cunts, out there!**

Brekk stands, shocked by the level of anger that has arisen within Cerrick. He also can't help but notice he can nearly see a breast through her loosely buttoned shirt.

Cerrick : **We are running out of time. There is lots to work out. I've got to get back up to the site and…fuck, get some rest.**

Brekk : **There is one thing?** (Cerrick raises an eyebrow) **If Ariff is 'The Chosen One', will I be able to take his place? I mean, you know, 'The Chosen One'!**

Cerrick : **Again, don't let their language fool you. He's just the 'Pertinent One'. Just enough understanding and charm and stupidity, to be used and then manipulated. Which is why you're a much better choice.**

Cerrick smiles at Brekk, inducing a little confidence in him and he manages a relaxed smile back at her. He's not sure if she blushes.

Brekk : (seeing that she is getting ready to leave, he desperately affects another slightly less convincing confidence) **Hey, listen. You know, it would appear I'm about to be a big thing around here so I was thinking, maybe you...**

She interrupts...

Cerrick : (stern) **No you weren't thinking. Don't be a prick, Brekk**
(angry) **Fuck. You're supposed to be convincing me that you're the right man for the job. That my efforts are worthwhile.** (Angrier) **Fuck!**

Brekk : (panicked into honesty) **No, no...I'm sorry. I don't... I don't know how to say what I want but I, I, um, I like you. And I just wanted to say that. Let you know that.** (he looks to the floor) **I'm sorry. I didn't mean to be so,** (he lets out a sigh of self-recognition) **creepy. I am sorry.**

Cerrick : **We don't have time for this.** (she sees how forlorn he looks and waits a moment for his gaze to tentatively meet hers…) **Apology accepted. Get some rest. Find a way to be relaxed with what is about to happen. I'll be in touch when I know what's going on.**

Seeing he is still upset she smiles a little encouragement and holds it until he manages to smile back. She nods and turns for the door.

Brekk : (Before she is gone) **What are you going to do?**

Cerrick **: I've no idea.** (looks concerned) **Everything has become so rushed.**

The door closes, and he is alone.

He sits, despondent.

A loose end. He considers some self-abuse, but finds he can't be bothered. He swigs the last generous mouthful from the tankard and drops backward onto his bed.

Falling into the eternal softness of his duvet he seems to hover in comfort while watching the hands on the loudly ticking clock blur around its face and he stares, mindlessly, at the soaring, fuzzy, second hand as the increasingly loud ticking and tocking crashes throughout the small room.

He wakes with a start. Someone is at the door. He looks over at the yellowed clock; he is woozy and his sight blurred but it appears to say 4.00am.

The door creaks open and silhouetted against the bright landing stands Cerrick, scantily clad and sexier than he would ever have imagined.

She glides across the room and into his arms,

Cerrick : **Hello my lovely**

Brekk looks mildly concerned, but she grabs his hand and puts it to her breast, and he can't believe his luck.

A Plan? Sunday 31st

Brekk wakes alone.

His eyes spring open as he flits through his memories of the night before. He remembers a breast and kissing, a fleshy bottom, and some sweaty effort. He also remembers the effort of pulling in his belly. He can't quite work out what was real or dream. He looks at the clock and is startled to see that he has slept through until the early afternoon. He jumps from his bed, alert to the fact that he will soon, probably, have something messianic to do, and he waits.

The time drifts slowly by.

His initial panic turns to bewilderment, then boredom, then…concerns start to fill Brekk's thoughts. Perhaps Cerrick has gotten into trouble…

The frustration is broken by the sharp trilling of the phone downstairs. Brekk steps toward, then puts his ear to the heavy door, and he waits to hear the call picked up. To his surprise, the phone goes unanswered before falling silent.

Desperation fills his mind and he is wondering what to do when it rings again.

He creeps from his room; he tries to be quiet but urgency forces his pace. His eyes dart about the passages and rooms until he finds himself downstairs at the desk, staring at the heavy, ringing receiver.

Wide-eyed, he looks around the reception area until, content he is alone, he grabs the handset.

Strange voice on the phone : **Oh, hello. I was hoping to speak to the gentleman staying at your establishment.**

Brekk : **Cerrick?**

Cerrick : **Brekk?**

Brekk : **Yes! Where are you, what's going on?**

Cerrick : **How'd you answer the phone, where's Lilly?**

Brekk : **I've no idea. There's no one here!**

Cerrick : (to herself) **That's odd.**

Brekk : **Where are you?**

Cerrick : **I'm at the site. You have to get here. Quickly.**

Brekk : **The same place?**

Cerrick : **Yes. Can you get here?**

Brekk : (he realises his recent panicked meanderings have given him enough insight) **Yes.** (he glances at the clock behind the counter) **But it'll take a while.**

Cerrick : **Just hurry and don't get seen.**

Brekk : **Why, what happens if they see me?**

Cerrick : (impatient) **I don't know. Just don't be.**

Brekk : (So many questions!) **What about my clothes, what should I wear?**

Cerrick : (angry impatience) **I don't know, Brekk. I don't know. Look, just get here and we'll work it out…**

Brekk : **But what about the...**(she cuts him off)

Cerrick **: I don't know, for fucks sake. Look, I know they're already preparing Ariff and it won't be long before he's put in the Rebirthing Maiden. We have to get to him before he goes in.**

Brekk : **The fucking what?**

Cerrick : **Just get here, Brekk.**

Brekk : **Yes, yes.**

Cerrick : **And you have to find the tunnel doors. I think I can let you in at 7oclock. Okay? On the dot.**

Brekk : **Um, okay. On the dot!**

Cerrick : **I've got to go.**

Brekk : **What about...** (the call is unceremoniously ended)

Brekk looks at the handset in frustrated disbelief.

Brekk : **Fuck!.. Tunnel Doors? Fuck!**

A blast of inspiration and Brekk runs to his room grabs his trousers from the top of his hold all. There in the pocket is the illustration from the police station and he studies it quickly. The position of the house foundations and a dotted line denoting the position of the tunnel doors is clearly marked amid the basin of the valley and the barren hill tops. He stuffs it into the pocket of his fresh trousers. Brekk checks the time on his wrist watch, and grimaces at the encroaching deadline. He meanders back from his room and down the stairs to the lobby and welcome desk. He struggles with some internal resistance, looks back to the stairs and thoughts of the relative safety of his room but turns back to face the door at the end of the corridor. He gurns as he wrestles with his reticent thoughts but he starts to walk.

He wades through his confusions and toward the door of the cottage where the crisp cold air seizes at his lungs and a plume of heavy misted breath precedes his exit from the doorway… then he is out along the stone pathway. He takes the steps down onto the tarmac and looks up to the darkening skies. His features harden as intent rises within him; it crystallises and feeds from previously untapped reserves of determination.

A light breeze freshens his cheeks. An intent, rarely explored by his physical side, courses through his veins.

A few deep breaths and a short gasp, his intent and destination set, he starts to run.

His heart pounds as he pumps and stretches his legs along the tarmac, then cobbles, and he feels himself slicing through the air as pulsing blood scours his veins and energy erupts from every pore.

Around the corner from the B+B, doubled over in painful breathless exasperation, Brekk, gasps for oxygen.

Brekk : (breathless) **Fu, cking,** (breath) **hell…** (deep breath...deep breath)

As he struggles for air, a sudden panic forces him against a scaggy hedge. A careless, speedy pick-up truck, its bed full of unusually attired passengers in the full swing of exuberant exhibitionism, bustles by. The scant garb that adorns the passengers' seemingly oiled torsos would suggest some pagan or supernatural affiliation and Brekk, between gasps of air, surmises they are headed for the same event that he is.

The truck and passengers pass noisily into the distance as Brekk bends back down to resume his asphyxiated distress.

A few lungfuls of air and Brekk straightens to a horn blast that startles him back into the hedge as another weirdo-laden vehicle tears along the road. It passes and Brekk steps out of the hedge to watch its loud bumpy progress into the distance. He takes a few more deep breaths and starts a less energetic trot.

Heavy clouds converge in the distance as the light from the lowering sun forsakes the evening.

Running, of any sort, doesn't seem to suit Brekk, so he has settled into a half walk half shuffling jog. Alert to the steady stream of passing vehicles he no longer stops but slinks into the shadow of the hedge line. A screech of tyres brings both a passing vehicle and Brekk to a juddering halt and, alarmed, he looks up to ascertain the cause of their concern.

He pulls himself tighter into the shadows.

Voice : **There he is.**

Breck, startled, shrinks down into a ball. He hears a stumble of limbs as some of the passengers dismount and their footsteps quickly near.

Voice : **He was there...**

: **Where'd he go?**

Brekk tightens as footsteps approach.

: **Here he is!**

Footsteps approach the coiled Brekk.

: (soothing tones) **S'all right, mate. D'you wanna lift?!**

Brekk exhales as relief relaxes his contraction and he opens his fear-clenched eyes. He looks up into the visages of two rotted corpses—his eyes spring wide as his mouth drops open…

Corpse1 : (reaching for his flapping chin) **It's a mask!…Fucking hell...**

Corpse2 : (also removing his rubbery face) **Ha, ha, fucking hell. You alright mate?**

The two, 'normal' young men help the recovering Brekk to his feet and brush him down in an affectionate act of easy comradery.

: **There you go mate, good as new. D'you wanna lift? We guessed you were going to the show.**

Brekk : (regaining a semblance of composure) **Uh, um.** (he checks his watch and again grimaces at the rapidly nearing deadline)

Bouncing along in the back of the open backed truck, Brekk struggles to hold himself upright, despite the fact he is sitting with his back to the cab and wedged between the two friendly guys. He is ignoring the chatty fellow to his right while he scrutinises the other of his fellow travellers.

The two young men who have helped him aboard seem, to Brekk, to be genial idiots and he has quickly dismissed their inconsequential ramblings. There is another male sat quietly against the tailgate and next to him, Brekk guesses, his female partner. Their pagan garb, slightly tatty, woven materials, worn and a little soiled, seems authentic. He watches with interest, noting their concern as they examine some small stones they are trying to cast amid the ructions of the bumpy ride. She is especially disturbed by the reading she has taken and is trying to instil in her partner the correct level of distress.

To their side, sitting along the flank of the truck bed, are two more young men. One of them seems to hold the crusty couple in extreme contempt and the other is trying to distract his blatant distaste.

Diplomatic Bloke : **Nah, this is gonna be a big one. My guys from Smokey are coming up an evryfing. You can have my pop if you like. Keep you going till we find 'em.**

Judgemental Bloke : (he looks to his associate) **Yeah, yeh, awright.** (his critical gaze refocuses on the girl and her partner) **What the fuck's wrong with these tits?** (shouts to the couple at the back) **You're off your nut, you lot. What's wrong with you?**

Pagan girl : (she stares savagely at the ingrate) **Why the fuck are you even here? You don't know anything, and you're so stupid you're proud of it.**

He is taken aback at her lack of intimidation and they stare at each other until everyone else's nerves begin to squeak. Brekk pulls himself tight against the cab and shrinks downward. One of the friendly masked guys calls across to the antagonist,

Zombie face : **Hey, where are you from?** (the antagonist and his friend glance his way) **We're just here for the tits!**

Judgemental : (a leary smile and he relaxes) **Ha, ha, yeah we were promised tits!**

Zombie face : (nods toward the girl who has now gone back to studying her stones and mouths silently…) **Bit serious.**

Judgemental : (loudly) **Fucking idiots**.

Brekk is still trying to shrink into the cracks in the truck bed but he watches the other incumbents, aghast at their attitudes. The couple at the back are much more interesting and as they travel, he sees their concerns have not diminished. She seems convinced that something is not as it should be…

They round a corner which has everyone leaning heavily against some centrifugal pressure.

The truck is slowing as it slides on mud and lurches through an open gate, then onto the soft ground of a field that has been disorganised into a makeshift carpark. Vehicles of all kinds are vying for space and excited partygoers mix with becloaked and dishevelled worshipers and practitioners of varying sorts as they swarm through the stodging traffic.

Moonlight bathes this festival of the bizarre and Brekk looks on, wide-eyed, before he is alerted into action as some of the guys in the truck jump to their feet and leap from the slowly moving vehicle. As they land, one of the masked travellers calls back to Brekk.

Zombie face : **Coming with us? We got gear.**

Brekk doesn't know how to respond correctly but looks to the couple at the back of the truck to see what they are planning. The girl is still studying the stones as a look of disgruntled confusion clears from her features and she looks up to stare directly at Brekk.

There is an accusing clarity to her glare and Brekk finds an internal explosion of guilt his only response. Panicked, he leaps from the truck, knocking past the masked zombies as he dives into the busy crowd. The girl stands, dumbfounded but pointing toward Brekk as he scurries awkwardly through the masses.

Her frustratingly tacit concerns, as is their target, are unnoticed by all present. She turns to her partner, who has just stood up; her look demands action but he has none to offer and he shrugs his lack of agency. As she looks back out into the crowd her eyes dart wildly as she searches for a glimpse of the fleeing Brekk.

Brekk, stooping as he runs and eyes wide in panic, wrestles his way into the strange and disparate mass. As he is consumed by the exotic swarm, the cold, evening air is displaced by the stifling heat of the horde.

He gains some distance and Brekk straightens as he barges, then slaloms, through the throng. He stops to catch his breath when, arrested by the sights of this fantastical gathering, a claxon and voice over loud speakers, reaffirms a countdown to the main event, and he is shaken back to his actual intent: the gates to the tunnel.

He reaches inside his trouser pocket and pulls out the torn piece of paper, unfolds it and looks, once again, at the schematic from the police station. He looks around at the hilltops and turns the paper to align his bearing.

He looks over his shoulder, peering through the milling freaks, satisfied no one seems concerned by his presence. He takes another deep breath and starts to walk.

A raised voice amid the crowd and he shrinks down again. Glimpsing a discarded mask trampled into the muddy grass he grabs it and holds it to his face. He straightens, looks quickly around him and then waddles, in an unconvincing attempt at nonchalance, deeper into the thick and excited crowd.

Brekk's confidence grows as, now anonymous, he weaves through this fantastic congregation. He slows and draws a breath as he takes in the wonder, awe and excitement that flows throughout this confluence of exotic folk. He slowly winds his way, eyes widened by the sight and sounds of these proud outliers, the fiercely unusual.

The magnitude of his goal, in regard to this congregation, suddenly seizes his thoughts and he stops, dead still, as the momentousness of the occasion claws at his very being. Is he to become their God? No, their messiah!?

He drops the mask and his hand falls limp to his side. His breathing is suddenly difficult. In his ears the noise of the revellers slows to a twisted roar and then stutters to a beat, a melting tick, a fucked clock.

Time has stopped and Brekk's awareness of the moment is absolute.

He feels the energies, the very life force of all those who surround him. Reality, on hold, pulses about him and he relishes the eternity of it.

Eternity.

Eternity.

Eternity with these freaks.

Eternity.

His mind wanders to the glib ignorance afforded him by the girls and guys from whom he has sought interactions, the dull responses to his insightful inquisitions, the wasted lives of the vapid generation with which he bitterly shares his existence.

Eternity.

Oh shit.

Cerrick. He remembers Cerrick. A smile twitches his lips and he remembers her words through a haze of sentiment.

: **Someone like you. Someone serious. Someone who can inspire.**

Cerrick...

The dream shatters and his heart thumps and jumps as the sights and sounds and smells of reality crash through his meditation. The sensory overload quickly subsides as, somewhat befrazzled, he bends to grab the dropped mask. Glancing back at the torn page in his other hand, he once more begins to run.

As he ducks and dives through the crowds he continues to glance at the high horizon, using it as guidance as he slowly homes in on the location of the tunnel entrance.

Brekk slowly adjusts his position around the approximate area. Expecting some fortified or heavily guarded entrance, he is confused at the lack of anything signifying the access to the tunnel. Frustrated, he looks around the scruffy marquees and stalls which are numerous.

Slowly, Brekk realises that the gates, previously within the cellar of the long-gone manor house, are now being housed and disguised within the erection of a tatty canvas food stall. It backs against another larger canvas marquee. Brekk tucks himself from sight and watches the tents for a while.

A little activity is busying around and inside the larger tent but the food stall has a closed sign propped against the protective food screen; except for a few disgruntled would-be patrons, it is devoid of life.

Brekk, waits until the frustrated and unsated sausage purchasers are moving away, then sidles up to the side of the stall and ducks through the canvas flap.

He sees the large marquee has direct access into the stall and voices of concern and organisation are close. Through a creased translucent plastic window he sees a mass of cabling and someone struggling with a public address system. Alone behind the greasy comestibles, Brekk spins as he determines to find the probably camouflaged gates.

He feels them underfoot, amid the trampled muddy grass. Two heavy hinged wooden hatch doors. He stares at them as he tries to grow the courage to reach down to open one, when the other yawns open.

Cerrick's face appears from the darkness of the sunken stairwell and Brekk can't help but allow a broad smile to stretch his cheeks.

Cerrick : (no warmth there) **Come on. Quickly.**

And she withdraws, out of the light.

Brekk, with no obvious options, follows her down cold and worn stone steps, into this unwelcoming unknown. Unsure of his footing in the gloom he turns to hold onto the steps as he goes. As he descends his skin prickles from the air which turns cool and moist.

At the bottom of the short flight he turns to be met by Cerrick's face, close and closing. Shock turns to hope.

Cerrick : (whispering) **Shut the fucking gates.**

She glances upward, dragging Brekk's gaze with hers. He understands and heads back up the steps. He closes the fucking gates and comes back down. Once again at the bottom of the steps he takes a breath, gathers a little optimism and turns slowly back toward Cerrick. There's no one there.

A receding voice from the void…

Cerrick : **Come on.**

Brekk, waiting for his eyes to adjust, edges slowly into the darker dark of what he knows, from the illustrations, to be a long, kinked tunnel.

As they move along the stifling passage a small flickering light in the distance increasingly throws Cerrick's form into a stark silhouette. He follows wide-eyed.

Cerrick : (calling back over her shoulder) **You weren't seen were you?**

Brekk : **No.** (he's surprised at how convincingly he lies)

Cerrick : **Good.**

Brekk : (best change the subject) **What's down here?**

Cerrick : **It's where they get him ready. Where he gets into the rebirthing maiden, apparently.**

Brekk : **Apparently?**

Cerrick : **Yes.** (Turning angry) **You can't just walk around here you know? Asking questions?**

Brekk : **Sorry. Um...** (Best change the subject again) **What's the rebirthing maiden look like?**

Cerrick : (a little impatient) **I don't know.** (then a bit more relaxed) **A bit like a coffin I expect. Now, shut up. Quiet.**

They continue in silence.

They reach the far end of the tunnel where a flaming torch is strapped to the wall, throwing meagre luminance onto an ancient wooden door. Broad knotty planks with heavy iron hinges stand between them and the mysterious destination. A small glimmer of flickering flamelight dances within the frame of a small grilled opening in the door. Brekk looks to Cerrick for inspiration as she edges slowly forward and slowly peeks through the grill.

Cerrick : **Excellent. They're not here yet.**

Brekk : (visibly emboldened) **Good.**

He pushes past her and opens the door with a confidence which deserts him once he steps into the circular cellar. Lit only by two more flickering flame torches the room resists scrutiny and Brekk's eyes struggle to investigate the space with nervous interest.

A circular stone-built room. The lumpen, heavy stone holds the bouncing shadows in a dark dappled camouflage. Two large, metal mesh doors take up a large part of the low dark ceiling which seems to squeeze the air from this dank unwelcoming space.

There, in the middle of the room, on top of an old, wooden block table lies a heavy, steel-bound, wooden sarcophagus, Brekk's senses are electrified by the sight and he is transfixed by his vague understanding of its importance.

There is a large rusty ring on each corner of the box and Brekk notices four heavy chains that droop from a large rusty gearing above which are stretched to hook onto hoops in the wall. Heavy weights hang against the walls of the room, attached by ancient rope to the gearing. It all seems designed to lift the wooden box through the doors in the ceiling. Brekk recognises the latticework of the doors from his earlier, panicked, investigations in the field above.

Looking around the dark dripping walls he can see a couple of wooden cupboard doors halfway up the wall behind the sarcophagus; they are bolted shut. A small worn stool stands against the damp wall. He discerns from the depths of the shadows two small doors on opposite sides, facing each other across the room. The doors appear to be held shut with bracing posts which rest in metal cleats that protrude from the walls either side of each door.

Outside, some heavy music, rhythmic and basic, starts shaking the foundations. Both Cerrick and Brekk glance upwards toward the noise. They look to each other, sharing an understanding of impending action...

Brekk : (A desire to start a conversation and he glances back toward the wooden sarcophagus) **Shit, has he got to go in there?**

Cerrick : **No. You do...You're not claustrophobic, are you?**

Brekk looks at her sheepishly.

Cerrick : **Look, we're going to have to hide until Ariff gets here.**

Brekk : **Hide, right...But then, how exactly do we get him to swap places with me?**

Cerrick : (This has concerned her too…) **I'm not sure. We're going to have to improvise...I mean, he's a nice guy…at heart. If you appeal to his generosity…explain why it's important to you personally.... um...and then of course, why it's important to the development of the coven… Engage his charitable side… I can try and help. I've been learning a charm.** (she sees Brekk's bewonderment) **It might help! We must try anything!**

While Cerrick formulates, Brekk, trying to be proactive, has found a long lump of wood on the floor in the corner of the damp stone room, and as he nods confirmation of her plan back to Cerrick, he is swinging it like a club, his own plan taking shape.

He practices bringing the lump down like a cosh and grimaces his intent to Cerrick who grimaces her unease back at him. Their eyes are wild with chaotic malcontent.

They search the room for hiding places but there are few nooks large enough to conceal a person. Cerrick approaches one of the small doors, pulls the locking post from its holders and leans it against the wall. She pulls the rickety door open and peers into the darkness; Brekk, taking her lead, has tentatively opened the opposite door. Like the other doorway, it is too dark to see what lies beyond. Cerrick calls into the terrifying abyss before her and the echo catches Brekk's attention as it hails from the darkness beyond the door he is hastily closing. She closes the small door and they both replace the holding posts as a nervous energy fills the room.

They both head back to the middle of the cellar, as he crosses the floor, Brekk anxiously checks the door to the passageway and sees that there is, as yet, no one coming.

Brekk : **look, about last night...** (He daren't look at her directly so he moves across to the sarcophagus and starts studying its carved form)

Cerrick : **I don't want to talk about it. Anyway I accept your apology.**

Brekk : **Not that bit...** (He looks directly at her but Cerrick is not interested and he purses his lips in frustration)

Brekk, re-finding distraction to be a necessity, continues to study the sarcophagus.

Glancing up the length of the sarcophagus he sees it has slit holes in the face of the lid, just big enough, it would seem, to see through from the inside, and also a small opening at the mouth.

Another slit, dagger blade size, is open above the heart. Ignoring the implication, he finds himself peering in through the eye holes, surprised to see a muslin sheet layered inside the lid…but there is also something beneath. The sarcophagus is not empty.

Brekk : (He jumps backwards) **Fucking hell...he's in there!**

The music outside has got louder and more frantic.

Cerrick rushes to the head and nudging Brekk aside, peers through the eyeholes.

Brekk : (whispering) **Shit, he's heard everything**...(louder)...**Ariff look, I know this sounds wrong but it really is for the best, if you really want this to succeed, the reformation, I mean…**

From behind his back, he hands Cerrick the lump of wood. She doesn't want it but Brekk is quietly insistent. He continues talking to the interned Ariff as he undoes the rusty clasps on the lid. He slides across the top half of the casket, as Ariff's head and shoulders become clear to them, he gestures to Cerrick with a downward thrust of his hand.

But Cerrick is studying the muslin clad figure more closely, she pulls back the sheet.

Brekk : (horrified) **Are we too late ?**

But no, Ariff lies serenely, at peace and snuffling as if in a sweet slumber.

Cerrick waves her hand in front of Ariffs face before prodding him gently, again gently. Then harder.

Cerrick : **Right, grab his head…**

Brekk looks out toward the door, down the long dark passage, shadows stretch and dance more vigorously at the far end of the tunnel.

Brekk : **Shit, I think someone's coming.**

As they lift him, struggling with his weight, his heads smacks on the corner of the table. They look at each other, a wince caught in their features, but he does not wake.

Cerrick : **He must be drugged!**

They look to each other in panic. Cerrick drops Ariff's legs and reaches for the closing bar to one of the small wooden doors. She tugs it open before rushing back to re-lift Ariff's legs. They drag him to the opening and pour Ariff's limp body into the darkness before Cerrick kicks the door shut and replaces the brace.

The soggy footsteps in the tunnel and the murmuring of voices are getting louder, closer, as above the music is pulsing.

Cerrick helps Brekk lift himself into the casket and drapes the muslin over him.

Cerrick : **You do believe, don't you.**

It is an order, not a question and as he's about to answer she puts her finger to his lip.

Cerrick : **You know it to be.**

The footsteps are near the door. She drags the lid across Brekk's still form and just before he is sealed in, he thinks aloud,

Brekk : **Why would he be drugged?**

But the lid is shut and the clasps closed.

Cerrick lunges for the other of the small wooden doors and pushing the closing bar from its cleats she opens the door just enough to dive in and she pulls it closed behind her just as the tunnel door creaks open into the room.

Cerrick sits in the darkness, tight behind the rickety door, looking through cracks in the old timbers. In strides Devvin, cloaked and his hood up over his head. He paces around the casket several times before approaching the head end and leaning down to whisper above the mouth-hole.

Devvin : **Hello, Ariff. Asleep, are you? Good, good…looking forward to this no doubt. This is a very important day, for us both. Immortality, it is a wonderful prospect. I'm probably one of the only ones who know...You should be proud Ariff, your spirit will live on. It will live on in me....it will be an**

honour to host your spirit, your vitality. (a glint of lustful fervour flashes across his features) **Your energy.** (he calms) **I will respect you Ariff. I will make you proud.**

He stands upright and as he walks around the case; he runs his hand down the casket, caressing the form sensually.

Both Cerrick's and Brekk's eyes narrow as they consider Devvin's words. Then Cerrick notices Devvin's hand. Older looking than she expected.

Devvin : **You know, you really are a blessing Ariff. The young and the stupid are so much easier to indoctrinate...but, well here you are.**

The door creaks open again and the two novice deputies step up to the threshold.

Devvin : (whispers) **Speaking of which...**

They bow slightly towards Devvin.

Devvin : **Ah yes, come in, do.**

They shuffle in, one drops a bag in the corner of the room by the door. It appears to be full of fireworks.

Devvin : (eyeing the deputies with a little disdain) **Yes. Very good.**

They stand before him, pensive.

Devvin : **All is well?**

Deputy 1 : (quite relaxed) **Yeah, I think so.**

Alarmed, the other deputy jumps in.

Deputy 2 : (injecting some decorum into the response) **All is well your Honour...My Master...** (he grimaces) **Um, Sir.**

Devvin : (ignoring the awkwardness) **Our friends are in place?**

Deputy1 : (influenced by his colleague, with a small bow) **Yes... your majesty** (Deputy 2's eyebrows reach for the ceiling)

Devvin : (bemusement) **And everyone knows what to do and when?**

Deputy 2 : **Yes...** (he settles on..) **...Sir.**

Devvin : **Very good.** (he pauses in expectation but nothing is forthcoming) **Let's carry on.** (still nothing) **Shall we commence with the precipitation?**

They realise Devvin's intent and cross the room to Devvin, who regally waits for them to get into position at his sides. Once in place a quiet incantation straightens the two deputies into solemn attention.

Devvin : **Right, excellent. Game faces, gentlemen.** (he remembers something) **Oh, I'll just go and change the music.**

1st deputy : **Oh sir, would you like me to go, I'll.....**

Devvin : **No, um...** (he sounds like this approach has gone wrong before) **I'll go...I can get a last look at the crowd. Yes...** (he starts toward the door) **What d'you think...** (he looks at the deputies from one to the other) **classical or that modern stuff?** (the deputies hardly react) **Yes, yes, I suppose, they do like that 'Drum and Bass' nowadays? Seems the days of Carmina Burana are well and truly over, and I do miss a heavy madrigal. Still there is that other one** (He again looks at the deputies) **You know, off the advert...** (they have no clue even when he starts humming) **No? Oh well, sign of the times I suppose, although what about that one—you know—with the Irish bit in it, livens things up!** (still blank) **No...well, we'll see. I never really know 'til I have to press Play.**

He leaves the room humming to himself.

The two deputies are left in the chamber and the first slumps onto the woodworm infested stool. The other, more furtive, moves to the door and watches Devvin amble down the passage.

He closes the door quietly and continues to watch through the grill. He looks back at the other, then leans down to the bag at the door.

He pulls from it a complicated leather strap which he starts to fasten to his forearm and then load with some of the smaller fireworks. From the chair, Deputy1 watches with interest.

Deputy1 : **Why d'you need fireworks anyway? Why not just use magic?**

Deputy2 : (frustrated at his colleague's lack of basic knowledge, there's an edge to his response) **It's a finite resource.** (then, less convincingly) **In ways.**

Deputy1 looks a little offended by the perceived rebuke, before allowing his next thought to dribble forth.

Deputy1 : (more optimistically) **So what do you think...? We could turf this joker out,** (he nods toward the casket) **me or you could jump in and uh, well, we could be shagging these birds for all eternity…**

Deputy2 : **If he hears you talking like that the only place you'll be for eternity is** (he nods toward one of the small doors) **down there.**

Both Cerrick's and Brekk's eyes are registering the conversation.

Deputy 1 : **Eh, Oh, no, man I'm only joking, ha! you know I'd never...**

Deputy 2 : **Anyway it wouldn't work.**

Deputy 1 : **Really?**

Deputy2 : **No,** (impatient disappointment) **of course not. It'll only work on Ariff.** (Cerrick's and Brekk's eyes narrow in some concern) **He is 'The Chosen One', 'The fucking idiot'. Can you believe it?**

Deputy 1 : **Eh, why only Ariff? Is he really special?**

Deputy 2 : **Well he's the one who took part in the initial part of the ceremony. That was the contract—a willing participant, believing and unafraid. What a clown. No, if you get in there the only thing you'll end up is dead 'ish'** ('ish', is punctuated with confused eyebrows) **and then in the cellar with the rest of the** (he makes speech marks in the air with his fingers) **'Immortals'.**

He nods again towards the small door, where behind, Cerrick looks over her shoulder into the ominous darkness. She turns back to continue looking through the gap.

The first deputy, having got up, is walking towards the little door, Cerrick leans back into the dark as he bends forward, picks up the locking post and wedges it firmly back into the holders, giving it a good hard shunt that shakes dust from the door and frame.

Deputy1 : **Gives me the creeps.**

Brekk and Cerrick are both quietly panicking, but unable to do anything for fear of being discovered.

Deputy 2 picks up the stool and strides back toward the centre of the room, dropping it by the sarcophagus. Stepping up onto the stool he tries to see through the mechanism, to outside.

Deputy 1 : **Have they started dancing? I don't want to miss that.**

Deputy2 : **Should be soon. He should be back by now. You know what to do?**

The other deputy nods enthusiastically which doesn't totally calm his superior's concern.

The music bellowing from up top has just ended and a new rhythm has begun slowly building. They nod to each other in approval.

Ah very nice.

Yeah. I like this one.

Behind the small rickety door, Cerrick squints into the cold darkness behind her.

Devvin strides back into the room as the two deputies assume their positions.

Again, the deputies bow slightly toward Devvin who makes his way around and between the two. He turns around and unbolts the rickety cupboard doors, and both deputies sneak a look in as the doors swing open.

Three shelves, all lined with black felt, are crammed full of silver and bejewelled antique items: goblets, jewellery, knives and daggers of ceremonial design. There are vials of oddly coloured fluids, bones and small skulls of unrecognizable creatures. A large, horned, head-piece sits in the centre.

Devvin reaches inside and pulls out a heavily decorated dagger. He again looks at the deputies with questioning, wide eyes. The first deputy shrugs; Devvin puts it back and pulls out a less ornate blade. The deputy gives a much more positive look and nods enthusiastically.

Devvin : **Good, good. I'll just check it fits.**

He turns toward the coffin and puts the tip of the blade into the slot above Brekk's heart and gives it a little poke.

Brekk, terrified, squirms.

Devvin notices a little movement behind the sliver of muslin that is visible through the slit and glances quickly to the 1st deputy.

Devvin : **Did he take the preparation?**

Deputy1 : **Oh, yes sir.**

He glances toward the second deputy, who nods back decisively.

Devvin : **How much did you give him?**

Again the 1st deputy looks toward the second.

Deputy2 : **All of it.....sir.**

Devvin : **Hmmm. We can't risk him screaming in the middle of it.**

He turns back to the cupboard and pulls out an engraved, silver wedge. Turning back to the maiden, he checks it for size and then gently teases it through the mouth-hole.

Pushing the muslin and wedge between Brekk's struggling lips, there is some resistance, so he grabs a heavy-looking goblet from the shelf and hammers the wedge home. He looks pleased with himself. The deputy's eyes widen, alarmed as blood seeps through the layers of muslin, darkening the cloth still visible through the gap.

Devvin : **Hmmm...you gave him all of it?** (he raises an eyebrow to the deputy, who nods emphatically) **Well, anyway, that should keep him quiet.**

Cerrick is staring, horrified, helpless.

Devvin replaces the goblet and reaches for the large horned head-piece. His head drops forward and he places the antlered skull-cap upon his head. He shuts the doors to the cupboard.

The deputies look at each other uneasily, then stand back to attention as Devvin turns back to face the sarcophagus. His mood has darkened.

Devvin : **Right. You two should go up, prepare them for my arrival.**

Without a word they march from the room.

Devvin : (loudly) **Aren't you forgetting something?**

The first deputy, embarrassed, reaches back into the room and picks up the bag of fireworks from the floor, then bows as he dismisses himself and is gone.

Devvin straightens and steps forward into a pool of light. Cerrick is startled by his appearance; his face is markedly older than before, his cheeks gaunt and eyes sunken.

Devvin again runs his hand over the sarcophagus.

Devvin : **I am sorry for your discomfort Ariff, I can assure you all...'physical'...discomfort will be ended shortly. Can't have you crying out in the middle of the ceremony, can we? Ruining it for everyone else.**

Devvin has noticed the juddering of the box and squirming of the incumbent.

Devvin : **I'm surprised at you Ariff. Have you really had such a change of heart? There is no way back. As you can see, I have expended a lot of energy in preparing this ceremony. I would have found a fool to fulfil this position but, by the grace of our forefathers, you walked in the door. You are special Ariff. I hope that gives you some comfort, some nourishment.**

Brekk : (trying to shout through the muslin and wedge) **o ghuu phplee aarm nu Arrff!**

Devvin can only hear the muffled noise.

Devvin : **No matter.**

He stands upright.

Devvin : **I am disappointed, but please don't worry, it makes no difference. In this practice a contract is a contract and you took part in it willingly. You'll be fine as soon as… Well, as soon as.**

He looks at the knife in his hand and smiles. He takes a deep breath, then adjusts the horned head piece. This action seems to inject him with an angry vigour and he stretches his jaw in an animalistic but silent roar. He stands upright, makes sure of his footing.

Devvin : (gruff) **I'll see you in a minute. Try and relax.**

Devvin reaches up and engages a part of the mechanism. The machine's workings tighten as dust falls from the rusty gears, which start turning and grinding before, begrudgingly, jolting into running more smoothly.

He rechecks his footing and braces himself, waiting for something. A crescendo of music and explosions comes from above and Devvin grabs at a small lever and is immediately sent, on a small wooden platform, up through a trap door in the ceiling and out into the ceremonial ring above. His appearance is accompanied by surprised cries of joy and loud cheers from the crowd before him.

Below, Brekk squirms, his attempts at screams muffled by gargled, blood-flooded sputterings. Cerrick is pulling at the door, trying to get her fingers into the cracks between the timbers, trying to shake the closing bar loose, but as it shakes it settles further into the cleats that hold it. She screams in frustration but there is no way through. She shoves her shoulder into the timbers, but they are stronger than they look.

Cerrick : (fraught) **I can't get through...I can't.**

Cerrick, behind the door, in the darkness, is consumed with terrified panic.

The Ceremony

Above the preparation room, in the moonlight, Devvin stands atop the scaffold platform, in the middle of the ceremonial circle, his arms outstretched, languishing in the worship of the gathered coven and their exotic associates. He has appeared before a scaffold dais, roughly made and draped with a richly decorated ceremonial cloth. The deputies stand to his sides. Around them dances a ring of naked worshippers. Behind them burns a huge bonfire and, in front of them, their audience. He looks out across the excited masses and bathes in their adulation. He looks out further and sees several of his closest, strangest comrades, watching, vigilant from a vantage point on the hillside.

His hands clench and unclench in time with the rhythms that resound about this feral arena and he slowly closes, then opens his eyes in blissful rapture. His gaze is drawn to some pockets of orgiastic engagement and a slim smile fractures his features, as under his breath, he whispers...

Devvin : **My people...my people...**

...

Below, Cerrick, distraught, shouts through to Brekk,

Cerrick : **I'm going to find another way!**

She turns into the darkness. Her eyes have not yet adjusted, and as she steps tentatively forward the floor deserts her and she slips, then falls, down a short flight of worn, cold steps. Winded but unhurt, she slowly pulls herself to her feet…then freezes as, from somewhere in front of her, from out of the darkness, a low moan breaks the silence.

Cerrick : (tentatively) **Hello...**

She reaches out and slowly edges into the black. Again, the moan.

Terrified she keeps heading forward.

Cerrick : (whispering to herself) **I'm coming Brekk... I'm coming.**

She is consumed by the dark.

...

In the field above, the stark firelight casts heavy, flickering shadows across the staging and dancers. While the deputies are drawing mystical symbols in the air, the dancers are reaching a crescendo of gyration and Devvin, snapping from his blissful distraction steps forward, away from the dais, to address the crowd. His eyes widen as he looks upon the infectious debauchery before him. His smile is wide as he begins to speak and the gathering quickly falls silent…

Devvin : (wild eyed) **We...are all Gods!** (loud and fevered endorsement explodes from the crowd. He waits for it to abate, then continues...) **And, we are all but grains of sand...Humility and sacrifice will allow us to recover and release the powers within. *You* are the power that drives this renaissance, this resurgence of our old religion. And you, and your patience, and devotion, will see that power—the god we all hold within—walk freely upon the earth once again.**

He looks out at the heaving bodies amid those more attentive to his words...

Devvin : **Yes, yes.** (relishing the carnal expressions. He looks away to the broader crowd) **Enjoy your time, for there is hard work ahead and our resolve will be tested as we build toward our final goal. So yes, enjoy the pleasures which you freely own**. (he glances again toward a seething mass of vigorous and sweated flesh, smirking at the sight as he watches his words influence more within the crowd. He watches, his breath growing heavy. He snaps from the indulgence) **But we are here tonight because the fates have decided to reward our faith, prove the worth of your commitment, and, see fit to bring our plans forward. Your efforts have conjured before us a servant of courage and faith...**

In the dank chamber below, the wooden maiden sits on the stone dais. Silent, but for the regular roars of the crowd above or the odd drips of moisture which run down the cold, mossy, walls.

The coffin jars slightly.

Inside, Brekk, wrestles with the constraint as he convulses in panic and fear. His garbled, bloody whimpers go unnoticed.

Devvin : **It is so important that these heroes are found and encouraged to come forward. Sacrifice of one form or another will be asked of all of us because... there is...** (he becomes briefly melancholy) **a war to come. But it is a war we must relish. We will battle to make the unenlightened accept and bow to our faith.**

(the crowd has quietened in the face of this grave proclamation)

Do not waste your sympathies. They will thank us as the light illuminates their path and burns the shadows and fear from their minds. We will need soldiers, those with the strongest faith and the most fervent desires, to achieve our goals. And you have delivered such a warrior to me. Willing to make the ultimate sacrifice he, as the brave few before him, will become manifest in the success of our campaign and become Immortal. Immortal within me! I transcend by the grace of these warriors...

...

Cerrick is tentatively feeling her way, virtually blind, into the unfathomable chamber. A small shard of light dimly illuminates what might be—Cerrick squints into the darkness—a door at the far side of the room. She stumbles toward it, then trips and falls against a jagged, mossy wall and into some soft baggage. She regains her footing, pushing back off the wall and the loose soft material. Her eyes are starting to adjust to the small amount of light and she looks up, into the dried, green, desiccated face of the corpse she has stumbled into.

She screams and falls. Scrabbling backwards, her nails and fingers graze and snag against the flinty cold floor. Stopping, her back pressed against the wall, she sits, breathing heavily, transfixed. Ahead are three corpses in differing states of decay. Though their skin is intact all that is beneath it is withered, a grey greenish tinge surrounding them. The bodies are, for some reason, manacled tightly to the wall.

...

Devvin : **We will never cease to celebrate these Heroes. And as such we must call to them in their idyllic plane. We trust they will enjoy our intrusion, even as we disturb their reveries to remind them of our eternal gratitude.**

The dead hang silently. As her eyesight adjusts further, Cerrick sits, shaking, on the damp stone floor and stares at the bodies, two obviously from younger children. The other the remains of someone older.

Devvin : **Now, call with me, my family...** (He spreads his arms inviting the crowd to join him in his exultation as he begins to recite Old words...An incantation, then) ... **The purest maiden, our daughter, Rowan, we honour you.** (once more, the incantation) ... **Our bravest son, Adam, we honour you.** (again, the incantation) ... **And, of our wisest Elders, Malwood, we honour you.**

Cerrick regains her breath. Then, as she remembers her intent, she gets to her feet. While trying not to look at these decayed bodies she slowly approaches, then creeps past to the doorway. As she nears, she glances at them, and they open their eyes. Dried, marbled, shrunken, cloudy eyes. She freezes as the cadavers slowly turn their heads towards her, dried skin and dust falling from the freshly mobile parts of their necks and they stare at her. Petrified, she stares back and waits...but nothing happens.

After a terrorized pause, she bursts into motion and lunges for the door which starts to collapse as it opens and she bursts through the splintering boards and lurches into another dark room. Glad to be over the threshold she looks back; a final look at the corpses and slowly her expression relaxes into one of pity. The three stare back at her and after a moment she drops her gaze and turns away into the coldness. As she does, from somewhere in the room she has just entered, the moan, once more, escapes from the darkness, but she has had enough.

Cerrick : **Right...**

She marches forward

Cerrick : (Determined) **Come on then, whatever you are.** (Then fearfully, imploring) **Where are you?**

She keeps going, flailing her arms in front of her. Another, louder groan, and she trips over Ariff. He groans again.

Devvin : **Now, my family, as Ariff is brought forth to the place of his greatest sacrifice I would ask of you to evoke your vitality, envigour your essence and release all negativity** (his vehemence demands action) **Free yourselves and enrich this holy place, this place of sacrifice, this place of rebirth, this place of raw energies...**

A new drumbeat has been slowly building from some hidden source and the crowd coalesces as it succumbs to the feral instruction.

As the crowd devolves into a seething mass, the two deputies step outside the circle to two winches which, after a synchronising glance, they proceed to turn. The rotations rattle the complicated array of chains, which travel up to the scaffold above and then down through the mesh doors to the chamber below.

The chains tighten.

In the chamber below the chains attached to the sarcophagus, taut now, begin to take the weight and lift the casket slowly towards the ceiling as the mesh doors are starting to ease apart.

Further below, in the darkness, Cerrick is wrestling with Ariff's limp form, half dragging him up a set of stone steps toward the small door. She realises this is a set of stairs and the door opposite to the one she had hidden behind and descended. As they struggle to the top of the steps, light shines through the cracks in the timbers. She kicks the door and they burst through into the preparation chamber as the coffin, holding Brekk, is creeping ever closer to the widening opening in the ceiling.

Cerrick props Ariff, who is slowly becoming aware, against the damp wall and lunges for the sarcophagus, scrabbling to undo the clasps. It is gently rising out of her reach and she shouts to Ariff,

Cerrick : **Please! ...help me!**

Ariff has no understanding of what is happening and looks on, bewildered, as Cerrick struggles at the slowly rising casket. It ascends out of reach when she sees, then grabs, the small stool and climbs onto it as the door in the ceiling opens. She stretches to grab at a rusty band, the stool collapses under her weight and she falls to the floor as the 'maiden' disappears through the ceiling and the hatch closes behind it, sealing the roar of the crowd from them.

Cerrick looks across to Ariff,

Cerrick : **Shit!**

Ariff : **What's happening?**

Cerrick : **It's Devvin. He's about to kill Brekk.**

Ariff : (incredulous) **What...why? ...Am I immortal?**

Cerrick : **It's a trick Ariff , it's all a trick.**

Ariff : **What...? No.**

Cerrick : **We've got to stop him Ariff! Now!** (she's frantic) **We've got to stop it now.**

Ariff : (looking towards the door and tunnel) **We'll have to go up.**

Above, the fever of the crowd has travailed the bowling rhythms and has arrived at its lurid destination. Devvin bristles with lascivious energy. As the sarcophagus nestles onto the dais and the chains loosen and drop away, the gathering has reached some moment of calm after-glow.

Devvin : (takes a few deep breaths but his speech is slowed by his delirium) **The brightest light, Ariff, has shown the qualities which will eventually bring our God to this earth. He has prepared himself and calmed himself in preparation for this his ultimate sacrifice. We shall continue in silence, as silence allows the earth to accept and deliver this gift to us all, and to this grateful messenger...**

From the outskirts of the multitude a bustling and noisy section have suddenly grown loud in their distraction and Devvin looks across to the lurking watchers on the bankside. He sees they are, to his annoyance, gone. He presumes their efforts are being put to good use but his anger is instant.

Devvin : (Screaming anger) **Silence!**

Devvin waits for the command to affect its mark, then recomposes himself and turns to nod to his deputies.

The two deputies, rigid with fearful formality, turn slightly to face out toward the crowd then drop to one knee and bow forward in practiced duty.

Happy with this progress, Devvin turns back to his own duties. With his fingertip Devvin scrawls some arcane symbols in the air above the sarcophagus. The symbols seem to light the air and hover a while, before fading.

Still breathing heavily, he pulls the chosen, ceremonial knife from a sheath under his gown and holds it up to the crowd, who release a quiet coo in deference. He performs more studied dexterities to the entrancement of his audience. A small flourish and he stops abruptly, teasing another gasp.

He looks out at those gathered, taking in the suspense of the crowd before slowly lining the blade tip at the slit above Brekk's heart. To some small alarm he notices the coffin jilt as, inside, Brekk still struggles in vain. Devvin's eyes narrow and he clenches his free hand…

Below, spying through the gaps in the mechanism, Cerrick looks at Ariff, panic and frustration etched into her features.

Devvin lifts his tightly clenched hand above the knife; he lines it up above the dagger hilt; he tenses for a hefty blow and with considerable force slams it down toward the end of the dagger. At the moment he is about to strike, he disappears.

For a short while there is silence. Then, from the crowd there are cries of stunned amazement and slowly this strange pause disrupts the mood, a nervous agitation rippling through the masses. The deputies turn, alerted by the reaction, and appear to catch the confusion as all begin to consider that something is wrong.

Suddenly, rising from the floor, the easily recognisable outline of the be-cloaked and be-horned Devvin reappears, and the deputies, their confused frustrations seemingly quelled, turn and drop once again. Another loud cheer bellows forth from the crowd.

Underground, in the chamber, Devvin lies in a crumpled heap.

He has been disrobed and Ariff stands over him with a long dagger pointed at Devvin's groaning uncomprehending face.

Devvin is coming to slightly, and lifts his face to look at…

Devvin : **Ariff?... ARIFF! What are you doing… who? ....**

Ariff thrusts the blade towards Devvin's neck.

Ariff : **You lied to me... You were going to kill me.**

Devvin : **Ariff, that's not true. You would have been immortal… Your spirit would have lived on.**

Suddenly, from above, there is a stamping resounding from the small platform. Ariff leans across, though he has little strength, and pulls the lever which brings the platform, along with Cerrick and Brekk, plummeting down into the chamber. They stagger as they struggle to stay on their feet.

Cerrick : **They're not happy... we should go…**

She is now holding up the dazed and traumatized Brekk, who is bleeding messily from the mouth.

Devvin : **Don't you see Ariff, they have tried to steal the ultimate prize from you, they want what should be yours, it's not too late.**

Ariff looks at Cerrick and Brekk suspiciously.

Cerrick : **Don't listen to him Ariff, if you want to see what immortality is like, look down there.**

She nods toward the barred door. Ariff, looks toward the door then back to Devvin.

Ariff : (to Devvin) **Well, should I look?**

Devvin : **Ariff .... what is down there is not important. You, your spirit would live on... It would enable me to continue with this great work that I... we have agreed is...**

Ariff, decided, shoves the blade up against Devvin's throat, silencing his defence, and then he looks toward Cerrick for some confirmation as to his next, potentially lethal, move. Devvin has started a panicked whisper...

Cerrick nods a confirmation to Ariff. He winces as he thrusts the blade forward, hard.

Ariff's thrust, although already against Devvin's neck, punctures nothing but air, and Devvin miraculously appears standing in the middle of the room.

Devvin : **You fool. Do you think YOU can hurt me? ...These tricks, do sap my strength Ariff, but what does it matter, once I kill you, I will be replenished, another lifetime of all this position has to offer. You could have been a part of this and in fact, you still will.**

Behind Devvin, Cerrick has grabbed and raised another knife and is about to thrust it forward, into Devvin's back, when he spins around and, with a flourish of his hand, she is thrown against the wall. Her feet hover slightly above the ground. She is held tightly and unmoving against the cold mossy stone. Ariff sees another chance in Devvin's distraction and, knife pointed, lunges. He is met with the same result as Cerrick, his body flung, then frozen, high against the wall. They squirm as they struggle to breathe...

Brekk cries out, his arm out-stretched; he is trying to counter the enchantment Devvin is using. Devvin stares at the effort; then, amused he laughs aloud and with another flourish of his hand Brekk is flung against the wall. The three are now held aloft, tight against the cold damp walls. Air is crushed from their lungs and they claw at their throats as they fight the tightening grip.

Devvin : (to Brekk) **You idiot , do you really think you can use magic against me? There is no magic in you, boy. Though,** (again he laughs to himself) **I do admire your belief.**

He turns toward Ariff,

Devvin : **Now, while I still have the strength...**

Devvin waves his hand in the direction of the cupboard, the doors spring open and another dagger floats from the shelf, as Devvin spins his hand the dagger follows the pattern, spinning in unison with his movements, and then as Devvin thrusts, his hand pointing toward Ariff's chest the knife shoots at great speed, like an arrow, for Ariff's heart.

Ariff rasps his last frightened gulp of air as Cerrick screams.

The knife stops dead in the air, an inch from Ariff's chest. Devvin, confused, looks around until, disbelieving, he sees Brekk, again with his arm outstretched, his eyes a picture of concentration,

Devvin : (disbelieving his eyes) **No... no... That's not possible....**

Ariff and Cerrick, through blood strained eyes, stare at Brekk, as unbelieving as Devvin.

Devvin : (increasing his efforts is proving futile) **No...What..?** (he collapses to his knees as his strength leaves him) **No, it cannot be.**

Ariff : (air suddenly refilling his lungs) **Brekk... how?**

But Brekk is concentrating all his energy; the knife at Ariff's chest spins in mid-air and slowly makes its way towards Devvin, gently alighting, tip up, under his chin.

Cerrick : (gasping desperately) **Ariff... Ariff!**

She catches Ariff's attention and nods toward the door of the chamber.

Ariff looks toward the door. Alarmed, he looks back to Cerrick. They both look to Brekk. Cerrick looks away.

Ariff : **Brekk... Brekk**!

Brekk : (sharply) **Not now, Ariff.**

Ariff : (more forcefully) **Brekk!**

He glances quickly to Ariff who nods, as quickly, towards the door.

Brekk looks quickly towards the door and has to doubletake. There in the doorway are three of the old ladies from the pub, each with an arm outstretched while simultaneously chanting under their breath.

Brekk starts to look slightly embarrassed; he still has his arm outstretched toward Devvin. He looks to Ariff, then back to Devvin. He relaxes his arm momentarily, just long enough to confirm his lack of any effect on either Devvin or the knife and a small grimace of understanding consumes his features. He drops his arm, again noting no effect on the knife and his embarrassment is complete.

Ariff, Cerrick and Brekk are all suddenly free of Devvin's invisible grip and they drop to the floor.

They stand slowly and they enjoy a few clear draws of breath as the old women move into the room to surround Devvin; their chanting rises in volume and intensity as they close in on him. Another of the women edges past to direct the three from the room and they quickly compose themselves before, without looking at each other, they file past the witches and out of the room. First Ariff, then Cerrick, then Brekk. Brekk is clipped around the back of the head by Lilleth, the last of the Witches in the doorway.

They quietly walk along the corridor; the cold echoes of their footsteps resound about them.

As they emerge from the damp passage their subdued senses are somewhat resurrected by the sight of the dark and fantastic masses being herded, contained and subjugated by the rest of the old women, now aided by several other esoteric groups.

Cerrick and Ariff look on in awe-filled bewilderment at these other magic-wielding swashbucklers. Both also notice Brekk's disconsolate indifference as they walk away from the melee.

Bathed in cold moonlight and framed by the heavy star-scape they walk off toward the village: stunned, silent and somewhat forlorn.

Cerrick is bursting with the urge to console Brekk but she sees from his shrunken demeanour that now is not the time. She resists the impulse, biting her lip as empathy clutches in her chest and she prickles with guilt as they amble along the dark roads. The noises emanating from the site slowly fade into the distance, leaving them only with their thoughts.

The three weary, bewildered walkers approach the outskirts of one of the small, hill-nestled villages and are unfazed as one of the little, becloaked old ladies emerges from the shadows to greet them.

She approaches Cerrick and whispers something to her. Cerrick nods in understanding before stepping away from the guys. A couple of steps and she stops then turns to look at Brekk.

Cerrick : (Gently imploring) **Brekk. Brekk...**

He cannot find the strength to look her in the eye. The old lady coughs her impatience and Cerrick, herself forlorn, slowly turns and walks alone into the darkness of the alleyway.

The old lady tugs at Ariff's sleeve as she heads off in a different direction and Ariff, then slowly Brekk, follow dutifully.

The van glides slowly down the street, Ariff behind the wheel. Brekk sits, lost in thought, in the passenger seat. The bright morning sun bleaches their view of the old village.

The old woman and her elusive sister from the B+B are out on the roadside tending to the shrubs above the low stone wall outside their home.

The van pulls up alongside them as Brekk unrolls the window. He notices some other folk in the garden and Lilleth is remonstrating with them despite their efforts to help with the ground and garden work. He peers intensely to see if any of them are Cerrick. But no; it is the two pagans from the back of the truck that took him to the site, and the girl who had led Ariff to the sacrificial pyre. The two groups eye each other with intense interest as the vans' engine chokes to a stop and the old ladies turns toward them.

Lilly : **Oh, hello lovely.**

Shem : (she looks up to consider the occupants of the van) **Oh, this is the young man, is it?**

Brekk : (he eyes this other old lady with some scrutiny) **Um, we just wanted to say goodbye, and check, you know, that...**

Lilly : **Don't worry lovely, we'll take care of everything. You'll eventually forget what you've seen here. Though if you ever want to stay again be sure we'll be glad to see you.**

Brekk : **Um, Cerrick, is she here?...I'd like to say goodbye.**

Shem : **She's not here at the moment lovely... but I'll tell her what you said.**

Brekk : **Listen the other night, in my room...**

Shem : **Oh, I wouldn't know about that lovely.**

Brekk : **But what happened... was it Cerrick... or!?**

Shem : **What do you believe happened my lovely, isn't that what's important?** (she turns away)

The van pulls off as Brekk rests back in his seat, his eyes afire with consideration. Ariff leans across Brekk to wave to the two old ladies. Smiling, they casually wave back as the van pulls away along the street.

As the van rounds the corner at end of the lane Brekk leans out of the window and shouts...

Brekk : **No! The truth, the truth is what's important...**

Shem : (she doesn't lift her head from her chores but smiles) **Okay lovely...okay.**

—The End—

Brekk and Ariff return in

The Shadows of Time

Arthur's Gold

and

A Fountain of Gods

Printed in Great Britain
by Amazon

29964861R00126